Spunk

Spunk

A Fable

HELEN O'REILLY

To my mother, who told stories, and my father, who told lies.

(Or was it the other way around?)

ACKNOWLEDGMENTS

Jimmy Moore and Pattie Moore-Schmidt, my brother and sister; with all the love I have in my heart. There is no one else like either one of you.

Mrs. Rose de LaFuente, Sister Marie Lurana, OP, Sister Christopher OP and Sister Frances Marion, OP (Amityville Dominicans). Diagramming sentences . . . . Who knew?

Paul Lynch, kindergarten crush. "In literature as in life."

My erstwhile teachers from York College, CUNY, living and dead: Drs. Paul Ray, Richard Nochimson, Alan Cooper, Daniel Coogan, Pat Franko, and Elayne Feldstein; Messers. Christopher Lehmann-Haupt, David Ignatow, and Stanley Kauffmann.

Carmen R. Sorvillo and all the other Sorvillos, especially my sons, Paul Jude, Matthew John, and Michael James. (And Tabitha, Sarah, Damien, Scarlet, Collin, Clementine, Amy Rose and Tesla Mae.) And Paula. Namaste. Thanks also, Anthony Catalano, my "bonus son."

My beloved (and too-soon departed) John Joseph Patrick O'Reilly and our Uncle Matt McGinn, and all the other McGinns, the living and the dead.

William John Coombes, "the Ancient Badger," who showed me the way to write at traffic lights, and let me come to his sett when I needed a place to do some of my own writing.

My inestimable colleagues, past and present: Nancy Schenck, Eliza Tutellier, Patrick Hughes, Daniel Kaelin, Dan Mager, and Valerie Killeen. Sonya Headen, Thomas Moore, too. My Scholastic teachers, editors, mentors, and friends: Liza Charlesworth, Jaime Lucero, Terry Cooper, Claudia Cohl.

Janice Montoya, Patrick Casey, and Nancy Jensen; my trudging buddies.

My HP, who through me does every good thing I get credit for.

And above all, thanks to the encouragement, love, inspiration, and support of my one and only, Kim Catalano.

TABLE OF CONTENTS

PART I

THE FORCE THAT THROUGH THE GREEN FUSE DRIVES THE FLOWER

PART II

THE GREAT WINGS BEATING STILL

THE FORCE THAT THROUGH THE GREEN FUSE
DRIVES THE FLOWER

The force that through the green fuse drives the flower
Drives my green age; that blasts the roots of trees
Is my destroyer.
And I am dumb to tell the crooked rose
My youth is bent by the same wintry fever.

The force that drives the water through the rocks
Drives my red blood; that dries the mouthing streams
Turns mine to wax.
And I am dumb to mouth unto my veins
How at the mountain spring the same mouth sucks.

The hand that whirls the water in the pool
Stirs the quicksand; that ropes the blowing wind
Hauls my shroud sail.
And I am dumb to tell the hanging man
How of my clay is made the hangman's lime.

The lips of time leech to the fountain head;
Love drips and gathers, but the fallen blood
Shall calm her sores.
And I am dumb to tell a weather's wind

How time has ticked a heaven round the stars.

And I am dumb to tell the lover's tomb
How at my sheet goes the same crooked worm.

—Dylan Thomas

CHAPTER ONE

SENGA THE CRONE

W HEN THE WORLD CAME TO, IT CAME, NOT TO ITS senses, but to its madness. Those who were left alive learned what their true needs were, which was almost as important as learning how to get them met.

Oxygen, of course, then water, then food. Those who were left alive were at the mercy of place, and some lingered long enough to learn how to get their needs met in the place where they were; others did not, and died. Still others began to travel the broken roads, to band together, to become victims or victors. Eventually, life resumed its potent, inexorable pulse.

And eventually, the things that had been left behind began to become "just the way things are," as if nothing had happened.

The crone's name was Senga.

She lived with the others in what had been, back when such descriptions had meaning, as the "largest contiguous oak forest in North America." It had gotten larger since it was so described, crawling over the places where the grand, transformational roads, built to endure by the great Robert Moses, had broken, when the earth underneath them was overturned and upthrust.

The trees had begun to reclaim their dominion quickly, growing down into the shallow valley toward Jamaica Bay, encroaching into the neighborhoods that had been Woodhaven, East New York, and Cypress Hills. They swallowed Glendale, Middle Village, and even Bushwick. They grew an isthmus joining what had been Greenwood Cemetery with what had been the northeastern fringe of Prospect Park, and Prospect Park they joined with Evergreen, Most Holy Trinity, and Mount Hope Cemeteries—connecting *them* with Forest Park and the north-looking swamp that had been Flushing Meadows. The trees took back what had been theirs, and in the taking, they also gave, not merely oxygen, but living room, raw materials, and a second chance for those, like Senga, who had been left alive.

She had known this place time out of mind, when men and boys had been plentiful and free, and she had had some of each. The first, she reflected, she had had in this forest, right here, close to where she and the others of her group now rooted and gathered, built and destroyed, changed little and grew less. "I breathe in; I breathe out. I keep on keeping on," she told herself. It was true, Senga went on. That was one of her powers.

She straightened up; she could still do that unaided, and as she looked around, she sniffed the air. It smelled green and alive. Not as alive as it had that one night—there had been stables nearby then, and the horses gave off a rich, brown smell that she'd known was warm hay and steaming manure. Because it was his first time, too, and he was mindful of all the stories that were told in those days to keep the young ones off each other and out of places like this, he took her deep into the darkest part of the forest he could bear to be in himself without being unmanned, entirely. He took her and she took him.

She hadn't fallen pregnant that time, so they went again and again, sometimes returning to the stable hill, and sometimes to places more or less exposed. Senga sighed in the now, and wondered: *was I a bad girl, or a shallow girl, or just a girl, and a young one, at that, to leave him so quickly? I thought I'd have all the time in the world, to have all the men I wanted. Well, I certainly got the time . . . .* She laughed at her own joke, and her face creased and cracked into a thousand sunburned wrinkles. Her white teeth were still numerous and healthy in her pink gums, and her hair, which had been a rich auburn-gold, was now the color of pale straw in the sun. She

16

knew she still possessed the ravages of her beauty, and sometimes she thanked the accident that had taken her eye—she imagined she knew how Medusa had felt the first time she turned someone to stone. *That was a good power, too.*

Senga needed all her powers, especially the ones that she didn't really have, but that she looked as if she might have. It had been many years since that day when the world had convulsed, and Senga was tired now, and felt herself weak, sometimes, and fearful. *It had been about 1971 when it had happened,* but she wasn't sure what year it was, now. It was hard to keep track, the way things had turned out. She scratched her chin, and wished she had a razor. The two or three whiskers that grew there seemed to sprout to a length of an eighth-of-an-inch overnight, and they itched like hell. She scratched her chin and asked herself the same series of questions she'd been asking herself for the past fourteen or so years; the ones that started with *what was I thinking?* and rambled around *I must have been crazy;* on bad days veering too close to *what if they find out,* or even *what if they already know?* and crashing to earth somewhere near *what'll happen to her when I'm gone?* There were days, more and more, lately, when it seemed likely that last question was about to be answered sooner rather than later. Senga figured that she had been somewhere between twenty and thirty in 1971, and she thought she was in her sixties, now. (Actually, she was fifty-nine and three-quarters.)

It was quiet in the forest. Shielding her eyes with one freckled hand, she whisper-shouted, "Pink!" There was a movement in the woods off to her right, so deft and delicate it could only have been Pink. Only partially satisfied that the girl was safely hidden, Senga signaled her to stay that way, and went to see what was being so unnaturally quiet that it was quite as much of a disturbance as a noise. *I don't care how much she begs, it's not worth the risk to bring her out here like this! It's not worth what it does to my nerves.*

She trusted Pink to stay hidden, to fully realize, without having fully learned, the terrible danger of being discovered. For fourteen years Senga had hidden her, and for fourteen years Pink had pressed upon Senga's thoughts. *I guess this is motherhood,* Senga thought. *I thought it would be different. Everything else is.* But Senga was right; it was and had always been the nature of motherhood to cause a woman to consume herself in care over the creature whose existence depended upon her competence, her capacities, her diligence and attention to duty. That couldn't change in thirty, sixty, or a hundred years. But Senga knew she had made it worse for herself by what she had done. She knew the rules, and she had disobeyed. She had kept a child of her own, against the rules. She had gotten away with it this long, against all odds. *How much longer?* she asked herself. The answer was always the same: *Not much. Will I be ready? Will she?*

CHAPTER TWO

PINK

PINK SHE WAS NAMED, AND PINK SHE WAS, PINK AND creamy white, her pale skin gold-spangled with freckles, like constellations of stars. Her limbs were strong and rounded, as was her torso with its short waist and broad shoulders, the whole crowned with a blazing, copper-colored mass of unruly curls that had never been cut; an untidy areola of fire and snap, from the midst of which her face, which could be sly or sweet, poked its way out. Pink.

She had come to Senga as a chick, an unwanted thing, from her own mother, a younger-than-her years girl full of superstitions and other fears. That had been more than ten years ago, maybe closer to fifteen. Pink had a blemish. When her eyes began to lose their universal, newborn cloudedness and their own, true color emerged, her young mother noticed the defect, and it terrified her. In her infant's eyes, which were now grey, now green, there was a streak, or a stripe, that was distinctly not-green. It was golden-brown, blazing out from the black sun of her pupil like a flare, or maybe a freckle.

The young mother's name had been Maureen, Senga thought she remembered. "It's not right," Maureen had said, worriedly pointing out the blemished eye to Senga, who'd brushed the young mother's dirty finger away from the infant's face. She glared at the young woman as if in angry amazement that something so stupid could live. Maureen had a mother of her own somewhere, but she was a lost and toothless drinker of dregs and findings; used-up, crazy, and soon-to-die.

It was not her own drunken mother, but Senga Maureen had sought when her pains began, and although the poor girl was clearly deficient, she must have known that to do so was against the way of the group. And Senga knew better, herself, but her by-then ancient, coal-bright anger against Hagar, the Abbess, and all of the others made her ignore this rule, as she ignored so many other rules. She had allowed Maureen to stay with her that night and labor. If she didn't make too much noise, it would be okay. Senga had no plan. But she had always been contrary.

Senga was old, and had delivered many women of many children, though none of her own survived, and it was she who had delivered Pink. Maureen had been young, and although dimwitted, was well-formed; a girl of sixteen or so with almost-fully filled out hips. Senga had built up the fire— her quarters at that time were deep in the dark part of the forest, and night was falling. That would have to serve as a veil. Besides, Senga thought, if Maureen was laboring now, it meant her cohort would also be near term, and the midwives could very well be busy monitoring them and maybe even delivering one or two babies this night, as well.

So Maureen, who would become Pink's mother and abandoner, spent her laboring hours and would spend her postpartum days and nights in Senga's quarters, until the baby, whom she had not yet bothered to name, had looked up at her one evening as she was feeding, and in her eye was the strange mark. Maureen yelped, and jumped, and pulled back so quickly her nipple popped out of Pink's toothless mouth with a sound like a sodden cork, and a spray of milk that might have spurted five feet in the air. Senga took the baby, and gave the distraught young woman some tea to help her sleep, and shook her head. She made shushing noises, and put a cool cloth on the young mother's head, and held her hand until she slept. *Poor dope,* she thought, *poor dopey girl.* Senga drank the rest of the tea herself, and slept soundly, too. The next morning, Maureen, the young mother, was gone, and the oddly, perfectly-imperfect baby remained with Senga. *You are*

Pink, Senga thought, *and that's as good a name as any.* From her cache of dented cans and not-too-badly broken boxes, she would make a kind of formula for the newborn to drink, mixing sweet, tinned milk with water from the bubbling streamlet that flowed past her shelter. Of course she had no bottle, and no rubber nipples, so she took a clean cloth and soaked it in the heated mixture, holding it against the baby's lips until it learned to suck the fluid out of the cloth. And so she kept her foster daughter alive.

Something was wrong in the now. Senga caught Pink's attention, and signaled her silently to get down, *fast;* Pink caught Senga's signal and nodded, then lowered herself— swiftly and silently—and flattened herself into the mossy ground, until the tall ferns that had bent to let her lie down sprang back up, and covered her, red hair and all. Senga watched the ferns bounce, and hoped it would seem to any observers that a rabbit had jumped there, and caused them to move. She stood still, or as still as she could with her heart leaping out of her chest, and waited. Whatever-it-was that was wrong moved closer. Senga waited and watched.

Mere stillness was Senga's camouflage—her stillness, her equanimity, and her age—over the span of her life the tawny skin of her body had faded to the color of her present surroundings, to pale gold and pale brown, and her clothing, when she wore any, was some subtle, variegated, leaf-color. She was wearing green clothing today, and had a brown burlap bag over her chest, for carrying things. Senga knew the

22

secret of being unseen when it suited her, and noticed when it did not. She waited. The silence became less silent.

The woods that had swallowed up most of the land between Brooklyn and Jamaica Bay kissed the eastern shoulder of what had long ago been called the Harbor Hills moraine, named longer ago than even Senga could remember. Where she and Pink had been scavenging that morning, the forest floor undulated, its topography alternating between moist fossae and bulbous, moss-covered hillocks. There were low hills and rock outcrops beyond, and everywhere, trees. Honeysuckle and Morning Glory snaked their ways up along dead trunks. Bees drifted lazily in the mote-filled sunshine, and an insect of some kind droned. Whatever was coming that had caused the forest to go silent was itself now making a racket, and was evidently unafraid of being heard, but because of the way the path wound around Kettledrum Hill, whatever-it-was couldn't yet be seen. Senga sniffed and moved out onto the path but did not signal Pink to emerge from her hiding place under the ferns. She could not do that. Ever.

Pink was watching, though. Watching Senga, listening to the rackety whatever-it-was, and feeling the leaf-filtered sunlight on her back, smelling the living earth under her hands. She smiled. "I'd like to eat this earth," she thought. It was dark and dense and smelled like the living thing it was. She dug in with her fingers, breaking through the velvet layer of moss, until her fingers encountered the dark, damp, dirt and her nose caught the deep, inviting aroma of earth, which she

23

knew well and loved. Removing her fingers one-by-one from the soil, she popped each one into her mouth to lick off its loamy residue of grit. If Senga had seen her she would have struck the hand out of her mouth and wrinkled her nose, but Senga was very deliberately not looking at Pink. If Senga had been looking she would have muttered something about "pica," and "germs," and "vitamin deficiencies," and Pink would have rolled her eyes, but Senga was determinedly not looking.

Peering harder through the leaves at Senga, finger in her mouth, Pink shrugged. She thought Senga worried too much. "If there was really something wrong, we wouldn't know it until it was on us. She told me that herself, a million times. Anyway, it's late in the day to be worried," she smiled to herself. Her speech, learned from Senga and practiced only with Senga, contained numerous quaintly outdated turns of phrase.

As Pink watched Senga, and Senga watched the road where it curved around the Kettledrum Hill, whatever-it-was came into view. Senga snorted in disgust and dug a balled fist into her hip, signaling Pink to remain hidden. Resolutely, she turned her face away from the spot where Pink had vanished under the ferns, and shook her head almost imperceptibly. *Girl Scouts.* Dangerous, but not in the ways they believed themselves to be dangerous. *Of course,* Senga scolded herself. *Which of the many hundreds of threats in this forest did you expect? Black Panthers? Tear gas? A race riot?*

24

The road as it came around Kettledrum Hill was narrow, but the Girl Scouts only ever walked two abreast, anyway. They were doing so now, a cadet in the lead beating time on an old firkin covered with stretched oilcloth, banging out the cadence with a heavy spoon someone had found and transformed into a drumstick. Only Pink and Senga ever called them "Girl Scouts," of course, and that was only a joke between the two of them. To themselves and their leader, the girls were "Maenads," the ragtag members of a gibberish cult, followers of the second-oldest of the women whose woods these were. She called herself Hagar, and considered Senga her rival, although the reality of Senga was such that even the idea of rivalry bounced off her. She was peerless, and if it had not been for Pink, she would have been utterly alone. For Pink was her foster-daughter, her companion, her surrogate, her prisoner, her hope, her madness, her folly, her reason, her despair, her hate and her love. And there were times when Senga realized these truths. And other times when she denied them. The others did not know that Pink existed. She belonged to Senga, and Senga belonged to her, as much as any mother ever belonged to any child, or any child to any mother.

Hagar came into view around the base of the hill now, and when she stopped without a word, her little troop stopped, too. She sighted Senga, and called to her. Senga growled under her breath. The Maenads, in their grass-stained white shifts, stood at something like parade rest. A few of them swatted at the clouds of midges that threatened to batten on them whenever they stood still.

"There you are," Hagar cried, assuming a smile that did not quite reach her eyes, as, arms outstretched, she approached Senga, who stood her ground and did not smile back.

"Here I am," Senga agreed, and suffered herself to be embraced without bending or returning the gesture. Hagar had her troop of "Maenads," but Senga had Pink.

"I heard voices," said Hagar, still holding Senga by the shoulders, still smiling her shark-eyed smile.

"You should see a doctor," said Senga, pushing Hagar's hands off her as if wiping off muck. She turned as if to continue on her way, adjusting the gathering bag hanging from her shoulder. "Seriously," she called at Hagar, over her shoulder.

"Very funny. I never noticed before; were you always this funny?" Hagar asked Senga. But the words fell against Senga's back and Senga imagined them dropping into the grass at her feet as she walked away. *Slowly,* Senga told herself, *and breathe. Do NOT let her see how frightened you are of your own anger at this moment. . . and do NOT look toward Pink . . . .*

A scream from the Maenads stopped both of the older women from whatever else they would have said or done next; froze them, in fact. A wild-haired Maenad, Yuki-Kai, twenty yards back along the path, near the foot of the rock called

Kettledrum Hill, was balanced on a small stump, arms above her head, stretching a thin, brown snake she held with both hands above her head, and it was she that the scream had come from, and it was echoed by another, from—*not Pink, not Pink, Heavenly Mother, not Pink*—but from Hagar's own girls, themselves all a little afraid of the wild Yuki-Kai at the best of times. *It sounded*, Senga thought, *like Mia*, a malnourished six-year-old who would have been completely unremarkable except for her ratlike face and ear-splitting shriek.

For her part, Yuki-Kai was grinning her gap-toothed grin and panting as she slipped the dead snake into her gathering bag and jumped off the stump onto the path before crashing away through the heavy underbrush. "Yuki," called Hagar. "Yuki-Kai," screamed the rest of Hagar's girls. But Yuki-Kai was quick, and strong, and ungovernable. Hagar shrugged, an "it's not important," gesture for Senga to see, and walked with controlled stride back up the path to rejoin her girls. *She'd rather I hadn't seen that display*, thought Senga. She shrugged, too, but she watched small, ratlike Mia, whose gaze lingered too long at the spot where Pink had been. *She can't know, can she?* Senga stood still and watched, arms akimbo, and saw Mia turn her little rodent face from the spot where Pink had been hiding to glare boldly up at Senga for as long as she dared before turning to follow the pack. Senga watched her pull on Hagar's sleeve, as children always do when they want to tell a secret. But Hagar, impatient to catch

Yuki-Kai, batted her away with the back of her hand. *Too bad for the little rat,* Senga thought, *but that was close.*

Oh, Mother, was that close. We have to be more careful. Actually, what we have to do is get the fuck out of here. Maybe the world isn't where we left it; but there's got to be something left that's better than here. How long will it be before we get back to whatever it is that's left?

CHAPTER THREE

MAENADS

HAGAR AND THE MAENADS POUNDED FRANTICALLY up the path along which Yuki-Kai had disappeared; they had to catch her. Not that they were afraid she would run out of the forest; the forest was altogether too big and alive for that to happen easily. It wasn't that there was no way out of the forest, either; there *were* ways, of course. Most of them led into the tunnels that had carried trains along the underground tracks; many came to dead ends; all of them were dangerous, especially the ones Senga had worked on and booby-trapped before she became too frightened by the dark to go on. There were paths, too, that led west, but none of the women had gone that way for many years; the miles of old burial grounds that lay there had not yet stopped giving up their dead, especially after each year's rainy season. No, they had to catch Yuki-Kai because they couldn't let her out of their sight, not once it got dark, anyway. Yuki was a prankster and a menace. She had to be caught before dark, or no one in their parts of the forest would be able to sleep.

Yuki-Kai had been born in the hatchery, one of the same Snatch and litter that had produced Pink. Yuki-Kai's mother, like Pink's, in fact, had been a Maenad from the Class of 1987, but unlike Maureen, Yuki-Kai's mother had stuck to her cohort. Unlike Pink's mother who had fled the group and found her way to Senga the night Pink was born—Yuki-Kai's mother now worked with Buffy on the Farm. She had no kind of relationship with her daughter—why should she have had? Most of the mothers had lost interest in their daughters soon after the daughters themselves had been born. Bearing children as they did, in groups, meant that new mothers nursed each other's infants indiscriminately. This communal wet-nursing meant that the infants were well-fed, but it also had the unintended result of impeding the formation of the mother-child bond, and set the tone for the future relationship. At least Senga had gazed into Pink's infant eyes as she fed her, and only her—had pored over her features and focused her intention and her intellect on the single child in her arms. The mothers who wet-nursed each other's babies talked companionably while the children sucked industriously and impersonally at their teats. Senga, watching them, would say to herself, "nothing personal," and chuckle at her own wit.

In the first few years, while the forests were still knitting themselves together and the women were still arguing about what had happened to them—in those days there had been about thirty women and girls in the forest. Of course, at first they didn't know it was only them, but twenty or so had been on each bus, and everyone except one driver had survived, at least for a while. If they had known what was about to happen to them, perhaps they would have paid better attention, but there was no way they could have known.

Later, when it seemed the world had come to a full stop, and no one was coming to their rescue, and they were the only ones left, some of them killed themselves. One woman killed her two small children and *then* herself. The others found themselves marooned in a creeping green jungle that seemed to flow as it grew around them, eating up ruins and rubble, covering whatever buildings had been in the forest with a kind of kudzu in a day, and re-creating itself to have dominion over everything on two legs by the time the first year had come full-circle.

By that time, as they always do, some leaders had emerged. Some leaders, some followers, and some fools. The surviving driver died suddenly (no one knew how; he had seemed to be getting better) but not without making his contribution to the ongoing survival of the group.

Senga, Buffy, and Hagar had been on the first bus, along with some *actual* Girl Scouts, members of the same troop, who had planned to attend the demonstration in order to earn something that had been called a merit badge. The scouts' caretaker, a nerve-thinned young matron from Flushing whose daughter had just joined the troop, had been one of the first to die following the accident; Hagar had assumed responsibility for them after that; she had been a schoolteacher, she said, and it seemed fitting. And that was the start of the Maenads.

The Abbess had been on the second bus with a dozen Guatemalan lesbians. The Abbess's name had been Abigail Barrow. (She lost her eyebrows from the heat of the fire after the crash, and they never grew back, which added considerably to her air of fearful abnormality as much as it did to her look of perpetual outrage.) The Guatemalans' plan had been to attend an abortion-rights march in Washington, DC, and their group had hitched a ride on one of their sister organization's buses as far as Manhattan. They never got there. In the forest their numbers were dwindling, as they would never take part in the Snatch, and in recent years they had kept more and more to themselves; you could sometimes hear their music floating through the woods, that was all. Predictably, the others called that part of the forest "Guatemala."

That's where Yuki-Kai seemed to be headed, with the Maenads and Hagar in hot, or in Hagar's case, flabby, mild, and arthritic pursuit. Senga signaled Pink to meet her back at the Relay Station. Senga would have to make her way there slowly in case she was watched. But Pink was watching Yuki, to see where she would go, although she thought she knew. She planned to get there first. As for Hagar, as soon as Senga was out of her sight, she flopped her haunches onto the nearest, flattest rock, and loosened the neck of her gown. She panted, and rested her hamlike hands, one on each of her knees, and looked around for Mia, whose canteen she grabbed to refresh herself. The rest of the Maenads came to a stop, too, and a couple of them swatted the horseflies that were still abundant here, near the stables, although most of the horses were long gone. "Well, girls," Hagar gasped, when she got the breath, "it's about time we stopped for class. anyway." A groan went up.

"No arguing—anyway, today you'll be learning about the Snatch." A bigger groan, in which more of the girls joined in, went up, but Hagar ignored it. Using the ubiquitous Mia now as a rather spindly crutch, Hagar tossed her gathering bag to one of the older girls and lugged her bulk off the rock. "Move it," she muttered, and move it they did, back toward the schoolbus that had been chopped and changed into a classroom-cum-dormitory. She would send a party out to look for Yuki once she'd had a chance to rest. No sense overdoing it.

* * *

There were other things that Hagar didn't know about, besides Pink. There were things that none of the women knew about any of the girls, not just Pink, and not just the wild Yuki-Kai either—that is the way it always is with young women.

For instance, Senga didn't know that Pink was aware of the boxes and crates of things Senga had found that were too dangerous to leave lying around, and too difficult to destroy. Pink knew about the bayonet and the hand grenades, although not what they were called, or what they could do. She'd found the box that contained them years ago, one day when Senga had gone to the old store at the edge of the woods; that trip could always be counted on to take a long time, sunup to sundown at least. Pink had looked into the box and had known not to ask Senga about it; she just knew she was not supposed to know. Of course, there are things that older women always know too, that the younger women haven't even imagined yet, but the young will never listen. That's another story.

Senga had tried hard to keep the secret of Pink, but as Pink herself was telling Yuki-Kai, "you can't keep a whole person a secret! *You* found me . . . anyone could."

Yuki-Kai shook her head and smiled sadly. "No," she said, touching Pink's cheek. "Not anyone. I was searching . . . no one else can search the way I can." The gaze she turned on Pink then was pure sugared love, but Pink didn't know that. Pink only knew for certain the things Senga thought she

34

should know; and she hadn't enough curiosity to find out much more for herself. She accepted Yuki's adoration as she had accepted Senga's care; she was beautiful: it was her due.

Yuki-kai was making love to Pink, as she had spied the older women doing. The tribadism of the others was, in the main, situational, like that of sex-segregated and sex-starved prisoners, or sailors of olden times out at sea. But Yuki-Kai's was real, and true. The needle on the compass of her desire would always find its true north in the arms of another woman; it was her tragedy to be in love with Pink, whose wan responses to her caresses stung Yuki-Kai with their pallid indifference. Pink's tragedy, if it could be called that, was that she was a "man's woman" in a world without men.

Of course, there *were* men, they existed. Outside the woods, in the Big World, which the older women sometimes called the World Before, pockets and remnants of men (and women) existed. Locked into itself as the forest was, nevertheless it seemed at times that the living woods themselves allowed them in. In recent years, though, fewer and fewer had made their way into the forest, and the ones that did were quickly dispatched. But as equals, as partners, potential lovers, or even and especially as friends; oh, no. Men in those forms and roles did not exist for the women in the woods.

Pink and Yuki-Kai were in the Fire Relay Station now, in Pink's quarters, toward the back. In the initial cataclysm, the building had dug itself into the slope of a quake-formed hillside, crookedly burying itself up to and almost over the second-story window sills in a mound of earth. When Senga had discovered the building some years after that, she had thought Pink less likely to be exposed there, so she and Pink moved in.

Pink had selected for herself out of the things Senga scavenged enough pillows, curtains, blankets, and even mattresses to make a comfortable nest out of that white-tiled kitchen that had served her as a nursery, a playroom, and a classroom, but that was now more and more a prison cell. Pink wanted freedom, and she did not believe Senga's warnings about the others, although even Yuki told her they were true. It seemed to her she was less free, not more, as time passed. It felt wrong.

As a child, Pink had been strapped to Senga's back in the loamy blackness of the tunnels near the Relay Station as Senga had explored and dug. She had been covered with clumped soil during cave-ins, and had held the foul-smelling, fast-burning, fat-candles in shaking, dimpled child-hands while Senga excavated and set her traps.

Senga had one fear; the dark. It dated back to she-didn't-know-when, but she had never been able to shake it off. Somehow to have the child Pink with her in the tunnels gave her some courage, as if having to care for a child took away her own thoughts of what might be alive in the smothering, menacing dark. However, the fear never left her entirely, and lately it had prevented her from digging much, at all. Their supply of candles was never enough—she would try to make them last by crawling down to the digging site without lighting one, but once any distance from the tunnel mouth, the pale daylight faded and the blackness grew deeper, thwarting her before she could begin to make headway in the digging. In the past few years, there had been months and months when Senga didn't dig at all.

Now, when Senga did dig, Pink—no longer a child strapped to Senga's back, but tethered to her by the same powerful, contagious fear—had carried the baskets filled with black earth back down through the tunnels and tipped them outside under cover of night, beside the Relay Station's back entrance, where Senga's garden grew, more lush and productive than any of the gardens of the others.

But Pink was becoming a woman, and she wanted freedom—now, not in the "someday soon" that Senga went rabbiting on about. The stolen outings, like this morning's, were not enough, although they were bought with endless wheedling until Senga gave in, and usually ended, as this morning's had, in near disaster.

"Senga is old, and half-cracked, but she's right about some things," Yuki-Kai was saying as she held one of Pink's outstretched arms in her hand, tracing endless figure-eights with exquisite delicacy on the upturned underside of Pink's tender forearm. Pink's lips were set, as much to express displeasure with what Yuki-Kai was saying as to keep from giggling; she was ticklish. The dead snake, in its bag-shroud, having served its purpose, had been forgotten.

The two girls were playing a game Pink had long played with Senga, that they called the "Pain Game." There had been times that Pink's ability to endure in silence both the kind of pain that ripped and burned and the kind so slight it could not be borne, like an itch—that ability had saved her from being discovered.

She was not in pain now, though, she was merely bored. She pulled her arm away from Yuki-Kai and flopped onto her stomach, pouting. "Really . . ." she turned and propped herself up on one elbow, shaking a russet curl out of her eyes and breaking Yuki-Kai's heart with her beauty, "what would happen if they found out?" Only the feeling for Pink that Yuki-Kai couldn't surrender made her answer tenderly for what must have been the hundredth time, "they would make you ride in the next Snatch. Then if you didn't get pregnant, they would make you ride again, or ride somebody else. Maybe somebody *worse*." Pink's bud of a nose crinkled with distaste, but she shrugged as if unimpressed, to tell Yuki-Kai, "so what?"

Now it was Yuki's turn to flop onto her back and laugh. "So: they're disgusting, they're filthy. They stink. They hurt, too. I don't know why they make us do it; why they need to, I mean. You'd think there would be some other way, but there's not. They say that's where we came from, so it's how the Goddess wants it, but I think that's bull. Anyway, you have to go into the cages, and pick one, and all the women get to watch. That's probably why Senga hides you here. She doesn't want you to have to go through all that."

Pink was silent now, imagining the cages, the fires, the faces of the girls and the other women, and herself among it all, riding better than anyone else ever had; face flushed in the firelight, triumphant. A flicker of anger rocked through her belly; what right had Senga had to decide? She would ride in the Snatch if she wanted! The thought pricked her, and a kind of hunger began to tighten like a wire, inside her, but for something that was not Yuki-Kai. Yuki-Kai, impatient now, rolled toward Pink, anger competing with lust within her. She grabbed Pink by the ankle.

"How do you know all this . . . ?" The strange hunger that was more than hunger vanished, and Pink's eyes narrowed.

She propped herself on both elbows, looking down between her legs at Yuki-Kai, who was pulling herself up the length of Pink's body.

"Everybody knows," Yuki asserted. "When you start to bleed, they tell you all about it, Hagar does, but by that time, you know already, from the other girls. Anyway, they don't do it in secret. The whole thing's right out in front of the Carousel." She began to stroke Pink's leg. Pink was not ready to give Yuki what she wanted yet. Pink wanted to hear it all, the whole familiar story. But Yuki was ready to go.

"You're exaggerating," Pink protested, but allowed Yuki's hands to resume their transit of her body from ankle to thigh; belly to breast. Yuki was dreamy-eyed; she was past becoming excited; she was young and she was *there*. Her breathing was shallow and her heartbeat, hard. Between her legs she could feel her pulse, faster and harder, insisting. She pulled herself on top of the languid Pink, who, as she ever had, allowed herself to be mounted. The girls stared at each other across the L-shaped space made by their bodies as Yuki straddled Pink and began to grind her hips against her. "You ride them like I'm riding you right now," she hissed.

Pink, supine, shrugged. She was indifferent to Yuki's love and to her sex, too, and she wondered what Yuki was feeling that she was not, what Yuki was seeing with her eyes-half-shut, and what she was doing that made the muscles of her thighs tight around Pink's thighs. Yuki was orgasming against Pink, grinding herself against the girl underneath her until another girl would have cried out, but not Pink, although her sparsely furred, plump little mound was being bruised by Yuki's furious orgasm. "Get off me," Pink grunted.

"It doesn't sound so bad," she threw in for good measure.

What happened next surprised them both, as Yuki bounced off Pink, reached down and punched her balled fist between Pink's thighs, piercing the dry membranes and unawakened flesh. Pink screamed then.

"It *is* bad," Yuki whispered, and rolled off, as the shocked and angry, bleeding object of her love curled around itself and moaned. "That's what they do that's so bad." She ran away, then, and wept.

Chapter Four

Screams

TO OCCUPY HER MIND AND KEEP FEAR FROM BINDING her steps as she took the circuitous and (she hoped) unsuspected way back to the Fire Relay station, Senga thought about the Driver. She had watched Hagar shamble off back to the buses, and she was ignorant of Yuki and Pink's deception. In her ignorance she believed the danger to Pink and herself was in being observed—she thought stealth was needed, and a seeming calm, so she pretended to a purposelessness she did not feel as she forced herself to saunter, to fool any observers.

The way she took was weed-choked, and what slender pathways there were were lined with sticky, spiky vines that snapped back when pushed, and stung where they caught flesh. Senga had encouraged them to grow, and they had until now served their intended purpose—to block passage. But now they worked too well, and Senga cursed Mia, and Hagar, and herself, and tried to bring the Driver into focus in her mind as she struggled forward. It had happened so long ago.

He had been tall, Senga remembered in the now, as she fought her way slowly up through the weeds, praying to the goddess who controlled the forest, if she would, to help her. She'd thought him handsome enough, with a face saved from perfection by a pronounced diastema between his upper front teeth. The women had kept him alive as best they could for as long as they could—he hadn't seemed terribly injured, but then he must have picked up an infection. Of course, there had been women on the buses who knew how to fend off infections, who knew how to get rid of headaches without aspirin, even how to set a broken arm or leg, but somehow nothing they did had helped the driver.

Senga had been the first to ride him; in those early days they had kept watch, and she had been eager to take the late-night to early morning shift, and what she had mainly watched for was any sign of an early-morning erection. Senga had had a theory in those days that a man would produce an erection even at the brink of death, even if it was only a pee-boner, and she turned out to be correct. *Hot damn.* She hopped aboard, but the ride was short and almost as rudely interrupted as the bus ride that had landed them here. It did what it was designed by nature to do, however; Senga fell pregnant. Buffy and Hagar fell in their turns. Strangely, each of them was surprised to note that the others had been doing the same thing as herself. At any rate, the driver, whether from his untreated wounds, from being ridden to exhaustion, or simply the realization that his future, if he should have one, would see him slowly and relentlessly turned into a flesh-covered skeleton attached to an erection, died soon after. It was never proven that it was Senga who was fucking him at the time; that was a story repeated by Hagar, who couldn't be trusted, anyway.

The women buried him. *Somewhere.*

(No one could ever really remember where, and so it became easy to frighten the young ones by waving a hand in the direction of something you wished to keep private, saying "up there, where we buried the driver." Senga had used this trick often to dissuade exploration of the old Fire Relay station until she no longer needed to use it; the girls' imaginations dissuaded them for her.)

The original proximity of the Fire Relay Station to the forest had not been in any way a response to a real or perceived fire danger from the forest itself. The forest was lush, green, and wet, and not in any particular danger of catching fire. But New York City had teemed with people in those days when the station had been built, and structures, old and new—some were more than a hundred years old and made of wood, some were newer and made of brick, but all of them would burn.

There had been underground trains then (although only the tunnels were left now), and trains that rode tracks in the air—"elevated" trains, they had been called. There had been two terminals—airports—filled with planes that rode the sky, two racetracks where men whipped horses to make them run so other men could wager on them, hundreds of tanks of gasoline, restaurants, taverns, and inns, markets for buying and selling, oil-storage tanks, Army-Navy stores and junk shops, and refineries and generating stations, too, rubbish dumps, wires, and factories, and carelessness, grudges, and greed; all the things that make human society fire-prone. It was a reminder that there had been a world of people who could endanger as well as save each other. The Fire Relay station was a remnant of that world's old technology as well, of people who worked as dispatchers, shouting into telephones, pulling switches and maintaining call-boxes, and it had been built to last. And last it had. But it was no longer needed to help extinguish fires.

There had, in fact, been a suggestion among the women in the very beginning to torch the forest, the better to see where they were. It was unclear who had made the suggestion, but it had the flavor of something Buffy would propose. To end the debate the Abbess said something about "not throwing the baby out with the bathwater," and the others had agreed with her; the forest would not be burned. They had also agreed that if they were to survive, they'd need to keep an eye out for at least two things: Buffy, and fires.

Much later, long, long after they had divided the food from the bus, and spread out and started living at some distance from each other, Senga had found and claimed the old Fire Relay Station for herself. It was a place where it would be easy, she thought, to keep secrets. So she had thought. And in a way, she had been correct.

Her thoughts of the Driver had done their job; they'd made her journey seem shorter, and helped quell her fear. She could see the back part of the Relay Station now, when she heard a thing she had never heard before; a thing, however, that she knew at once. It was Pink's voice, and she was screaming. Senga no longer cared who might be spying—she began to run.

CHAPTER FIVE

SCHOOL

"YOU CANNOT BELIEVE WORD THAT SENGA says."Hagar rapped the palm of one hand with the ruler she held in the other, dropping her words into the cadence kept by her feet as she paced around the circle of Maenads. These sat, with their legs akimbo, knees above their shoulders, and bits of mirrors in their hands, angled to provide them an instructive view of what, in Hagar and Senga's time, had been called "private" parts.

Hagar had put on a spongy pair of footwear she'd fashioned from the now-ancient bus-tires upon entering the bus-turned-classroom; their soles made noises as if they were dryly kissing and unkissing the worn-out linoleum floor of the bus. The girls stifled laughter both at the sounds and at the subject of the lesson.

What she had said was not simply an exaggeration born of dislike; it was true, Hagar told herself. Senga was past becoming . . . dishonest. . . if Hagar was feeling kind, she would say that Senga was becoming senile. Except of course that senility was a condition of age, and Senga was only a year older than Hagar, herself. So it wouldn't do to call it senility, and it wasn't quite dishonesty . . . it was secrecy, and failure to report, a lack of reliability. It had always been present in

Senga, ever since the crash. At least that was as far back as Hagar's knowledge of her went.

As time had passed and no help had come, and both drivers and some of the early survivors had died; and the Guatemalans took themselves off to another part of the forest, there had been left a group of nine adult women and eight girls in the woods. The girls had grown and had girls of their own, and those were the Maenads Hagar instructed now.

Hagar, the one everyone called The Abbess, and Senga had each carved out spheres of influence for themselves. Of course, Senga's only included herself and Pink.

In addition to watching for fires—which was a responsibility shared by everyone, really, more than a job, *per se*—Senga made and scavenged for paper. She had always been described as "down-to-earth" and "practical," and it was she who had, as soon as it became evident that they were going to survive, decided that they needed paper. Especially toilet paper. Even if they no longer had toilets; they would have toilet paper. "Women," she'd declared, "Need toilet paper." Hagar and The Abbess had looked at each other. "She has a point," said the one called The Abbess. So Senga began to scavenge, and one of the things she scavenged was paper.

Hagar founded the hatchery, where the Maenads would be born, and the nursery where the Maenads would be kept safe, and the Abbess took on the task that had been filled in the outside world by authorities, clerics, and mages. As for Senga, she walked, and as she did she scoured the forest floor for paper that could be salvaged, or pulped, or otherwise reused, for toilet paper and for the Abbess, too, who needed paper for record keeping, and Senga suspected, for other things.

Senga turned out to be a natural scavenger, and soon fashioned herself a gathering bag, then another, more elaborate one, with compartments for wet garbage and dry garbage, and toxic garbage, too. It was in this way, by scavenging, that Senga first noticed that the forest had a way of answering her needs, although not always in the way she expected.

There had been some hippie chicks on the buses among those who had lived, and who were almost gleeful at the prospect of what their "leader," Buffy, called, "livin' off the land."

Buffy had been a large girl with greasy, mouse-colored hair that she parted in the middle of her head and allowed to hang over her muscular shoulders. It grew down to her waist, and she had an unconscious habit of flicking it back over her shoulder with one gigantic hand while snorting as she lazily tossed her head. She had been standing hip-deep in a pool of water when Senga first saw her. *She looks like some kind of sleepy animal . . . like a . . . water buffalo*, Senga had thought, that first time. She told her so; and far from being insulted, the girl whose nondescript name had been Mary Ellen or something equally ordinary became the more exotic *Buffy*.

That pool of water had been a swimming pool, in the high school Buffy and Senga had attended together when there were such things as high schools. They had both worn short-sleeved, beige nylon blouses fastened with brown plastic buttons and pointed collars, and tight-fitting brown gabardine skirts, nylon stockings held up with metal garters and flat, white, pancake-shaped hats. White gloves and flat-heeled brown oxfords, as well. It was a Catholic girls' high school for teaching secretarial skills to young women about to enter what was called the "workforce." The uniform was an attempt to mimic what actual, ladylike secretaries in fact wore. It was an unsuccessful mimicry, filtered as it was through the consciousness of the dowdy, habit-wearing nuns who ran the school. The distortion of the costume was completed by the students themselves, who rolled their skirts thigh-high and in the name of "Women's Lib" went braless under their thin nylon blouses, to the despair of their frustrated teachers and the delight of the boys and men they passed on the way to school

Buffy had been one of those girls whose boyfriend was older, and had his own "place," a grimy flat above a grocery store where a flag with dirty, not-quite cream-colored, not-quite-white stripes alternated with red, and a blue field with stars that had once been white served as a curtain. Young people went there to "do drugs." Senga balked at doing anything more than smoking hash with Buffy in those days— Buffy's fingers were always violently filthy and stained with

God-knew-what. But it was common knowledge that Buffy attended class giddy and stoned, or sleepy and stoned, or spaced-out and tripping, flailing her hands at unseeable, uncatchable bits of what she called "space fluff." That was when she attended class at all. She and Senga lost touch after graduation, and it had been by pure coincidence that they'd ended up on the same bus, traveling to the same demonstration, in the same year.

Buffy had been traveling to the demonstration with a group whose members included Hagar. She had lost her teaching job and was working as an office manager for the Manhattan plumbing supplies company where Buffy had found work, upon graduating from that school for girls. The two women had become office friends, and when Hagar's hangovers threatened her job, Buffy introduced her to pot, which at least didn't make her so violently sick on Monday mornings.

"Where was I?" Hagar asked herself in the now.

"'You-cannot-believe-a-word-that-Senga-says,'" quoted Mia, the underfed, wizened *rat-girl*, whose stringy hair was tied up in two blonde bunches atop her head and from which strands were continually escaping. Hagar stopped squelching around the classroom and peered down the length of her own body to see where the little voice was coming from. Mia smiled up at her, baring small pointed teeth, and Hagar blanched and put her hand to her neck. If there had been a string of pearls there, she would have clutched it. She cleared her throat. "Yes," she said, and resumed pacing.

The girls were poring over the reflections of their genitals in the shards of mirror as Hagar spoke, goggling bug-eyed at one another's stuff and rolling their eyes in the time-honored manner of schoolchildren everywhere each time the teacher's back was turned. Did she really think they needed these sad little lessons to learn what had after all come so naturally to all the thousands of generations that had preceded them? Some of them had been playing not only with themselves, by themselves, for months—in some cases, years—but *with* each other as well, for almost as long.

Hagar hit the palm of her hand with her ruler again and again as she spoke, and resumed her wheezy, noisy procession. "For instance," she said, "Senga will tell you the strangest things about the part of your body we are examining today." As she squelched around the perimeter of the circle behind them, half-hypnotized by her own words and unseeing, they would make faces at each other, wrinkling their noses and crossing their eyes. Hagar, oblivious, droned on.

"She would tell you that that is where babies come from," Hagar sniffed," and of course, technically, or perhaps I should say, bio*log*ically, (she tittered at her own wit) she is correct. But first and foremost, the purpose of your *clit*-or-is (you see it there, at the top. At the TOP, Glynis.) is to provide you with pleasure, and it is secondary to the vagina, one might even say inferior to it, for that reason. The clitoris is the only human organ devoted solely to pleasure."

A shadow fell across the circle of bodies; it was Yuki-Kai, who stood, red-faced and panting, in the classroom entryway. "Don't I know it!" she cackled, grabbing her crotch with one hand and swinging into an empty seat. "Sorry, Miz," she said, and she almost looked like she meant it. The smaller girls, like Mia, looked from one to another, both frightened and excited. But the older ones, closer to Yuki-Kai's age, giggled. Hagar pursed her lips and exhaled through her nostrils. "Nice of you to join us," she smiled at Yuki. "It saves us the trouble of searching for you. This lesson is especially important for you and your cohort. The girls who have begun to bleed."

A moaning, groaning, giggling wave of that peculiarly female blend of gloating and dismay bubbled across the room. The "girls who had begun to bleed" variously smirked, or grimaced, or blushed. There were five of them, counting Yuki-Kai. Five who would take part in the next Snatch.

"We know all about it," said Yuki-Kai, wiping her eyes with her fist, and her fist on her dirty shift.

"Really?" Hagar's smile was cold. "Who knows *all* there is to know about the Snatch?" The girls hung their heads, and even bold Yuki-Kai was cowed into silence by the grim and knowing condescension of that "all." But Hagar was a bully, and she bullied Yuki now.

"Since you know so much, why don't *you* give the lesson, Yuki-Kai?" Yuki couldn't resist the bait. She rose from her seat and walked to where Hagar was standing. Hagar's nose wrinkled; she smelled sex on the girl, which was impossible, therefore to be ignored. Hagar squinted at the treacherous child, but said nothing, extending the broken ruler for Yuki-Kai to take, but the girl shook her head. Hagar closed her eyes and pursed her lips as if to say, "suit yourself," and sat down in the seat Yuki-Kai had relinquished. Mia the Rat-Girl squealed. Yuki-Kai glared at her; *the water is up to your knees, now. Might as well jump.* She shook herself and began.

"'The Snatch'," Yuki-Kai intoned, falling into the speech pattern Hagar habitually used when instructing. She began pacing with her hands clasped behind her, "is a ritual, but it is more than a dead, empty ceremony. It is life itself." She shot a glance at Hagar, whose face did not betray anger or frustration if either of those were what she was feeling. She looked rather haughty and proud, and a bit indulgent, all at once. Emboldened, Yuki-Kai went on.

"When we came to the forest, all praise to our Mother in heaven, we had been prisoners of patriarchy, and slaves to men." At the word "men" the girls shivered theatrically, and Mia let out a squeak. Hagar smiled tightly; they had learned well. "In her divine wisdom, and in her own divinely female way, our Mother delivered us from the dominion of men, and granted to us the freedom to choose our own way forward." Hagar allowed the merest wrinkle of a smile to crease her lips, and thought to herself, *Do I do that? She really is quite good.* She adjusted her large bottom on the rude wooden seat that had been made for a girl, and one half her size at that.

Yuki-Kai, having completed a transit of the lopsided circle of girls, stopped pacing at the end of it farthest from Hagar, and turned to face her listeners.

"The Snatch—it organizes our lives, and provides us with new life, and new women. We women are now, for the first time in the story of the world, quite literally, on top. We take from men the single thing they have that we cannot make for ourselves. And when we are done with them, they are done for good."

"Done for good," the girls in the circle chanted softly, in unison, and as they chanted they drew their small and grimy thumbs across their tender throats.

Hagar stood up. "Well done," she applauded. "Take your seat, Yuki-Kai."

But Hagar stood where she was, forcing Yuki-Kai to squeeze past her to get back to her own place, and then she addressed the girls again. "Yuki-Kai has learned well. As must you all. For your lives, and our very world," and here Hagar gestured upward and outward, a gesture that encompassed the entire forest, and, it seemed. to possess and enrapture her as she spoke in a voice that at least *appeared* to be tremulous with deep feeling, "depend upon how well you play your parts in this ritual that is more than a ritual—" and here she stopped, as if too overcome to continue. She began to lumber toward the exit, trailing small girls and bits of mirror in her wake.

"Time to remind Buffy to check the traps," she called back, her words straggling after her. "Mia?"

The Rat-Girl pricked up her ears. "Yes, Miz?" Hagar was in full sail, and didn't deign to look back at the child.

"Collect the mirrors and lead the Young Ones back to the dormitory. It's time for your naps." Hagar waved a vague hand. More groaning greeted this announcement, but the children had reasons to obey, and obey they did. "Yes, Miz," said Mia, to Hagar's indifferent back.

"I think I'm gonna be sick," whispered Glynis, as Yuki-Kai lounged next to her in the seat Hagar had just vacated. "Don't be such a baby," Yuki whispered. "What're ya, on the spout?"

Glynis shook her head violently, so much so that her teardrops scattered; one splashed Yuki-Kai's arm. Yuki wiped it off and twisted her lips in a sneer. "Pffft. Baby." She left the crying girl to dry her own tears and lit out into the forest. Another girl might have felt remorse at Yuki's treatment of Pink, her only friend, and her love, but not Yuki-Kai. Most of the softness had been twisted out of her by the time she was twelve, and she was fifteen now.

It was not just the idea of riding the men that made some of the girls feel sick before their first Snatch. It was a cascade of long-delayed realizations, some of them deeply disturbing to the more sensitive girls. No longer could they

56

avoid the knowledge that they would have to "ride" the men who had been captured for that purpose. (And although the older women never called it rape, that's what it was, and that's what it felt like—to the girls as well as to their victims.) If, as was the desired result, a girl fell pregnant, she would become a mother according to her body's readiness, not that of her mind or her soul or her spirit. Of course, some of the young girls' bodies might have begun to ovulate and bleed, but that was no guarantee that their hips were sufficiently wide to birth a baby. As even the youngest ones all knew, sometimes babies came late, or feet-first, or dead, and then there would be more and tenderer meat in the food pots. And of course, sometimes boy babies were born, and they went into the pots, as well. And it was too much for some of these young ones to countenance, but no number of tears would dissuade the Abbess, and Hagar, and Buffy, and the other women. It was the Snatch, and the Goddess Herself had dictated its terms, so they said.

CHAPTER SIX

SPUNK

GODDESS OR NO GODDESS, THE SNATCH EXISTED because there was a thing the women needed if their world in the woods was to continue, and the thing they needed came only from men—it was Spunk. Baby Batter. Skeet. Jizz. Semen. Man-milk. Splodge. Penis pudding. Ejaculate. Cum. Once the driver died, they couldn't get any, either. Not without leaving the forest or letting men in; and that they would never do. So in the very beginning, they'd had to decide. They'd had choices:

1. To assume that the world had lurched toward its inevitable Armageddon (except not quite), and that if they had been left alive, then so had others. Some of those others were

bound to be men. They could find them, and figure out what had happened, and set about the real business of surviving, which would include carrying on, procreating in the imperfect but customary way of humans throughout time. This was the choice favored by Senga. However, in this she was opposed by most, if not all of the others, notably Hagar and the Abbess, who favored what Senga called "door number two":

2. To assume that whatever had happened had happened just to them. That the world had come, not to an end, exactly, but to a fork of sorts. That yes, they were survivors and that those who had managed to ride the driver and fall pregnant would in due time give birth to children who could be raised as if in another Adamless Eden. The fact that they were cut off without communication seemed to some of them to indicate that they had in fact been the only ones to survive, and their own wishes led them to believe that this had been somehow intended.

"Think of it," Hagar had smiled. A world of women, and daughters raised by women. Without patriarchy or its oppression . . ."

"What," Senga had ventured, "if one of us—"she pointed to Hagar and herself—"has a boy." Hagar looked startled. "Why borrow trouble?" she asked. She had looked almost sweet then. Reasonable. "Each pregnancy has a fifty-fifty chance of producing a girl . . . why not assume the best?" They were sitting in a circle around the fire, smoking the last of their readymades, and Buffy was smoking something else.

"If it's a boy," she suggested, "you can just whack off its little thing. *Make* it a girl." She giggled and wrinkled her large nose, and made a snipping gesture, holding invisible scissors. "Wee, wee, wee, wee, wee. . . ."

Senga reached over with one leg and made contact with Buffy's rump, rolling her farther away from the fire ring. Buffy giggled as she rolled down and away, then stopped, then subsided into sleep, snoring gently.

"Think of it, Senga," Hagar's face was shining in the firelight, and with the glow of early pregnancy, her plain, broad face looked angelic. "Why not believe the best?" She pleaded. "Why not believe we've been given a chance to start over again . . .". She held out her arm, palm down, and swept it in a circle around them, indicating the fire ring, and the woods beyond, and the ruined buses. This was in the beginning, before the women had grown brave enough to separate from one another, and to move off to find the living arrangement that suited each of them best. The driver's body had been buried "up there somewhere," and the other immediate casualties, too, but the woods were still scarred where the buses had crashed, and the things that had been salvaged from the luggage compartments hadn't been sorted yet. The foodstuffs they had intended to donate once they had arrived at their destination were, providentially, non-perishable, by intention.

At this time, the women and girls still slept in a huddle around the fire at night, and only ventured out in pairs during the day. Those who were native-born Americans wouldn't notice until after their departure was well underway, that the Guatemalans had been disappearing, singly or in pairs, since the first few days after the crash. This all took place before they understood the depth of their isolation. There was nothing to threaten them, except of course, each other. But they didn't know that then.

"What makes you think we can survive for very long?" Senga had asked, incredulous. The force of her despair pushed her to her feet, and she winced. "Why would you even want to?" She demanded. The fire flickered and leapt, illuminating the women's faces all around her, blurring their hard edges, veiling even the ugly ones in a golden, firelit beauty. This light jumped and dazzled. It hurt Senga's already throbbing head. Senga put her hands to her temples and looked around wildly. "Do you hear yourselves? I mean, what would be the point of just surviving? Why not just finish the job? The world has ended; don't you get it?" The women gasped in unison, and a small girl shrieked. Senga went on, "We should be thinking about the best ways to off each other, not all this 'world of women' crap!" More gasping and shouts of "no!" followed, as the Abbess tried to restore order.

"Then what were you doing fucking the driver?" Hagar sneered. Senga stared back at her. "I don't really know. Not that I have to explain myself to you. . . . How about we just say I was getting laid, one last time, for old time's sake," she said, her voice rising. "What's it to you—did you think I was *trying* to get pregnant?"

Hagar's hands flew to her belly, as if Senga's words were blows threatening her gestating child. "Well, we're both pregnant now," she said. "I'll take that as a sign that the world is NOT ending. It's just ... changing."

"You . . . dope," said Senga. "Even if it is 'just changing,' this is a pretty radical fucking change, wouldn't you agree?" No one answered, though Senga was addressing them all. "*Wouldn't you agree?*" she asked, louder this time, gesturing toward the entire group. The forest swallowed up any echo. There were murmurs from the women, and even some clicking of tongues, but no answer.

The Abbess stood up and stepped around the fire to Senga. Her eyes could be soft and kind when she chose, and her voice was as calming as money. "Yes," said the Abbess, touching Senga's arm with the soft fingertips of her right hand, "radical, as you say."

"And how long do you think it can go on this way? How long can *we* go on?"

The Abbess had a high, sweet, tinkling silver laugh that raised the hairs on the back of Senga's neck, and she laughed as she said, "Another two thousand years, perhaps? Who knows? Long enough," and she placed her hand on Senga's still-flat belly "for the children you two are carrying to grow, to be born, and for a new world to be formed. Formed by US!"

Senga opened her mouth, then snapped it shut, then opened it again. It was too much. She gestured toward her own and Hagar's bellies. "I suppose we're gonna wait till these two grow up and get married and have a family . . . assuming they're boy-and-girl!"

"Geez, Louise," said Buffy. No one had noticed her wake up, and no one noticed her nod off again.

The Abbess came close to Senga now, and grabbed her above the elbow. "No one is pretending that men aren't necessary, Senga," she hissed, so the others wouldn't hear. "No one is saying they have all been killed, either . . . but look around you . . . it certainly seems that way. We just need a few. A manageable few. It seems reasonable to think that the Goddess we worship has heard the prayers of the oppressed women everywhere, across the world, and chosen this beautiful manner of freeing us from the scourge of a world dominated by men. Doesn't it?"

Senga was close to crying now, with frustration, and hunger, and anger, and pain and the horrible feeling of being the only sane person left alive. The crash had broken a bone in her foot, it was healing only slowly, and she hadn't had as much as a drink of water all day. Despite that, she felt desperate to pee, and she suspected she had a urinary tract infection.

The Abbess simpered. "Haven't you noticed we're in a forest? We can get everything we need, right here . . ." Senga was close to pulling her own hair out.

"It's a *forest*," she yelled, "not a fucking farm. And even if it was, we're not farmers." Beyond the firelight, Buffy had started to snore again. The Abbess clicked her tongue and was about to speak, when Senga said, "Don't you click your fucking tongue at me . . . before we think about anything else, if we are going to live, we need to find food. The stuff we brought won't last forever. We need to find water." She kicked at the candy-bar wrappers and cookie boxes that had come off the buses and that now littered the campsite around the fire-ring. "This crap is running low. . . . Don't you want to know *what happened*? We need to find out if there are other . . . . survivors . . . we need to see if they need help . . . or if they can help us . . . and we need to find the *men!*"

Hagar got to her feet. "Trust *you*," she sneered.

Senga took a swing, and connected with the side of Hagar's nose, but just barely, before the Abbess got between them, and Buffy's fellow stoners roused themselves enough to grab Senga by the elbows from behind.

"Sisters," the Abbess said, in her calming, soothing, money-voice, "sisters, we have all been through a terrible ordeal. Terrible and wonderful. We have survived. Miraculously." Senga shook off the stoners but she kept her head down, and rubbed the knuckles of her fist. She listened to the Abbess. Hagar wailed theatrically and held her hands up to her injured face. She was ignored.

"Go on, Senga," said the Abbess. "We *want* to hear what you have to say. After all, we're not men. We respect

64

every woman's voice." Senga glowered at her, but was forced in spite of herself to admire the way the Abbess was taking control of matters, even though she had a feeling it would not be to her benefit for the Abbess to have control over Senga, herself.

Senga exhaled heavily and swallowed before she spoke. "We don't *just* need men. I mean . . . . We need to find out things . . ."

"What kinds of things?" asked one of the stoners. Other women echoed, "what things?" A voice—Senga thought afterwards that it had been Hagar's—came out of the dark and said something Senga heard as " . . . only one thing!"

Senga looked around in the firelight at these strangers, these women she had not known before getting on the bus (except for Buffy, of course), and with whom she seemed destined to die. All they had had in common was a vague and well-intentioned cause, and now that their world had ended, they didn't even have that.

"We need to find out if there are . . . I don't know . . . horses, or dogs, or poison ivy—or snakes . . . running water . . . . wild animals. . ."

Murmurs of assent were heard in the leafy dark, and a thrill of fear went through the gathered group. "That's right," said one woman. "Right on" said others. "I saw a raccoon . . . they can have rabies," one woman started to say, but the Abbess silenced her with a glare.

"Go on," she said to Senga, in a voice like warm milk. "Tell us what else you think we need to know."

"You shouldn't need me to tell you what else—just think! Food, water, shelter . . . ."

"As I said before, we're in a forest. It can provide all these things, and more."

Senga stared at the Abbess in dumb amazement, and the air between them rang with their rage, Senga's white-hot and the Abbess's blue and cold. Abigail Barrow had been a refined and sensitive girl, overindulged by her Holocaust-survivor mother and a WASP stepfather who had spent their post-war lives spoiling their only daughter and running the largest and poshest department store in Queens, New York. She had studied art at Goucher College, in Maryland, but left before graduation to marry her boyfriend, who was being sent to Vietnam. *His* parents owned a bus company, and she moved in with them after he was deployed. When he was killed, Abigail lost the baby she was carrying, but got to keep the house her new in-laws had bought her and her ill-fated young husband as a wedding gift, in Forest Hills Gardens.

Senga had come from an insalubrious apartment house in Jamaica, Queens, not far from where the women now found themselves, had they known. She'd shared a bedroom with her siblings until she was eleven or twelve, and a bed with a drunken uncle on occasion. The roots of her fear of the dark were in that place, with its cavernous, dangerous cellars where bad people, strangers, and neighbors, and even uncles, did

66

forbidden and furtive things. But her mind would not let her remember the roots of her fear—the uncle who'd made her afraid of the dark was dead and buried, and only the fear remained.

Senga *was* aware of the chasm between herself and a woman like the Abbess; she marveled at the things she knew that the Abbess didn't, yet she also had to admire the social jiu-jitsu that had put the Abbess on top of the group here, as she had undoubtedly been in the big world outside. Senga sighed; where had *she* been the day that lesson was taught?

"The forest doesn't *provide*," she mocked the Abbess, shaking her head. "You have to work for what you need. You have to *take* it. And having men around would make the work a lot easier."

"Oh, of course, I see," the Abbess chirped. She was a year younger than Senga, but seemed older, and not just older; antique, or quaint—a throwback to an earlier age, an age of girdles, and lace gloves, and pearls. Afternoon card games and cocktails. "I think, dear," she said, crossing her arms over her chest," that you are deliberately looking at things in the worst possible light. I was speaking figuratively; of course we will *all* have to work; and while it's true that men's muscles would make that work easier, it's really not a fair exchange. We pay too high a price when we let them 'help' us." A murmur of agreement came from the women. During their brief acquaintance, Senga had already formed the impression that the Abbess was one of that class of women who would forever maintain their unblemished record of unwavering idleness, while simultaneously accruing accolades for their accomplishments. It was happening already.

The Abbess yawned, and her yawn spread throughout the group. "It's late," she purred, reaching out to stroke Senga's sooty cheek. "Everything will look better in the morning. We can all figure out what we should do then. I suggest we get some sleep, now."

Senga put her hand up to run it through her hair in impatience. *I need shampoo,* she thought, and began to laugh, although her lip quivered. "I need shampoo," she said aloud.

Hagar, about to bed down with the Abbess, turned and sneered, "Why don't you put that on your list? Right after MEN"

Senga sighed. It would be a long night.

Chapter Seven

Early Days

I T HAD BEEN A LONG NIGHT, AND IT WAS FOLLOWED BY A long day, and then a string of them. Once it seemed clear that they *were* alone, and not in any imminent danger of anything except starvation, they gathered confidence and began to spread out; just in time, too. So many women, so close together, and so dependent on each other will begin to fight, or at least split into factions. Which was what happened, eventually. But it took a while.

By that time, as they always do, some leaders had emerged. Some leaders, some followers, and some fools. Senga, Buffy, and Hagar had been together on one bus, along with some actual Girl Scouts, members of a troop who were planning to attend the demonstration in order to earn something that had been called a "merit badge." The scouts' caretaker, a nerve-thinned young matron from Flushing whose daughter had just joined the troop, had been one of the first to die after the accident; Hagar had assumed responsibility for the girls after that; she had once been a schoolteacher (or so she said) and it seemed fitting. That was the start of the Maenads.

The Abbess's real name had been Avigail. Avigail Rivka Bronfman. Her birth father had died the year she turned four, and her mother, left penniless, was forced to look for work—the stepfather would not enter the picture until after a decent mourning period. There was no pre-school, no nanny, no *bubbeh* or auntie to care for little Avigail. Hitler had seen to that. So one day, Rose Bronfman, survivor, put on her good wool-felt black hat with the sturdy little demi-veil, rubbed off her red lipstick with her hankie, straightened the seams on her stockings, and took her small daughter by the hand. She locked the door of the house she was about to lose to the bank, and walked hand-in-hand with her daughter down the big hill, looking both ways as they crossed busy Hillside Avenue.

They knocked on the door of the convent of the Sacred Heart on Parsons Boulevard, where Rose had made an appointment for tea with the Mother Superior. Rose's tea grew cold in its china cup as she explained to the Mother her plight. The Mother Superior's glasses perched lightly on her upturned nose, and their gold rims reflected the glint on the rim of the delicate china teacups. And the Mother smiled, a most understanding smile. Yes, the nuns could take care of the child. Yes, she could enter the parish school, though she was a year too young, and the wrong religion.

There would be a donation, a baptism, two baptisms, actually, for it wouldn't have done to allow a Catholic child to be raised by a Jewess. And the problem of who was to care for the little girl—who would be christened "Abigail"—while her mother went to work for the nice young Mr. Barrow at his Emporium, was neatly solved.

It had been Abigail Barrow Renton, a soldier's widow, who had organized the fateful bus trip, and she who had arranged to carry, as paying passengers, the Guatemalan women, some of whom were actually "radical" nuns, female religious.

The Guatemalans' plan had been to attend an abortion-rights march in Washington, DC, and their group had thought it providential when they managed to connect with their sister organization's buses to take them from the mother house in Amityville as far as Manhattan. They never got there. They didn't speak much English at the time of the crash, and that's the way they liked it. In the years following the crash they kept more and more to themselves, and several of the original dozen were now buried in the small cemetery they had established next to the chapel they had built out of stone they had found in the forest. It was rare now to come across them;

they kept to themselves, although you could sometimes hear flute music and hollow-sounding drums in the dusk, floating through the thick forest air from what the women referred to, predictably, as "Guatemala."

Hagar and the Abbess, strangers when they met, were natural allies and assumed the roles of leader and lieutenant. Buffy attracted a trio of like-minded pot-heads from among the survivors, and their first efforts toward meeting their own needs went into pot-farming. Emptying their pockets and turning out the seams, they scraped together a quantity of stems, and seeds that they managed to germinate between dampened paper napkins they found in the dead drivers' lunchboxes. These they planted in a wet, damp, overhung spot that Buffy deemed suitable.

Senga, out scavenging, came across her a few weeks after the plants had gone into the ground, looking worried. She was biting what were left of her grimy nails. "Man, I don't think there's enough sunlight here," she told Senga, pointing to the dug-up patch of ground which, Senga had to admit, was practically devoid of sprouts. "But it's not as risky."

"Risky?" Senga looked around. "Buffy, there's nobody here. No law. No pigs. Nothing. Dig 'em up and plant them over there." She pointed to a dappled clearing. Buffy looked at Senga in wonderment. "No . . . law. Huh. Right on," she said. Marveling, she stumbled off to uproot and replant her precious crop. In a year's time she would be stoned nearly constantly; a goal she had been striving for since the age of twelve.

Hagar commandeered the young girls, and together they righted and cleaned out both school buses, even the one that had broken in two. The surrounding area they cleared of brush and undergrowth. The bus that had broken apart they would use for classrooms; the other they used for sleeping in. They were large, modern "luxury caravans," built for comfort.

The Abbess and her Acolytes, the women Senga thought of as her "court" moved into what had been a derelict carousel and its housing. Most of the painted horses were intact, and the roof had been replaced the year before the crash, as part of some ill-fated Parks Department restoration. There was enough ventilation so that when they burned the damaged horses for heat on the concrete floor of the building, the smoke could escape through the vents. (They kept the mirrored calliope and the huge turntable and a few of the horses intact, as they gave them something to look at and listen to.) A playground nearby had survived, but just barely; the jungle gym was a twisted wreck, and the seesaws were torn apart, but there were still two slides, and a swing set that was usable.

Senga stood aloof and alone. She miscarried the driver's child within weeks of conceiving it, after a brief pregnancy marked by intense nausea and extreme fatigue. She kept her own counsel and she wandered through the strange and yet familiar woods; the first winter, she took slim refuge in a bandshell that had survived intact, but offered little shelter from wind and rain. She burned one hundred folding wooden

73

chairs that first winter; she'd found them stored underneath the stage, and burned them on the concrete apron of the bandshell, and she still almost died of pneumonia.

One day while scavenging, she would, in the future, spot the red tile roof of what would turn out to be the Fire Relay Station; she had driven past it a hundred times when the world was different and the woods had just been a part of New York City. But it must have moved from where it had sat on the crest of Woodhaven Boulevard. It would seem to have traveled downhill, coming loose from its fixtures and foundation and half-burying itself in a high hill of soft earth. *Perfect.*

But she had not found it. Yet.

CHAPTER EIGHT
MOON MEETING

P INK HADN'T EVEN BEEN THOUGHT OF YET ON THE day Senga found the Relay Station. That day itself was years away from the women's first days in the woods— those days and nights had turned to weeks and months and then a year, and then another, and both Senga and the Abbess had been proven right: the forest had sustained them, but they needed to work it. Of course, as also predicted, the Abbess didn't do much of the work; with her chosen coterie, her Acolytes, she dwelt in the ruined Carousel near where the buses had crashed when the world ended.

"I hear she pays a Guatemalan woman to come in and clean it once a week," said Buffy, and then she belched and began to laugh. She and Senga were in Buffy's encampment, itself at the edge of the forest on the shore of a strange-smelling lake, drinking hooch and sharing a pipe. In addition to her flourishing marijuana plantation, Buffy now had a distillery of sorts, where she concocted a degraded and malodorous variety of moonshine. Having no specific knowledge of winemaking or home-brewing, with only the ingredients the forest provided and the vessels that Senga scavenged, it was no surprise to Buffy that the stuff was vile—what was surprising was that it had not yet proven lethal. With no Campden tablets to kill wild yeast, some of Buffy's vintages were almost hallucinogenic rather than hypnotic. They produced a bone-rattling buzz and a wracking nausea. (Her experiments with making LSD never came to anything, although the woods were filled with Morning Glory flowers, which caused Buffy no end of tantalized vexation.) For psychedelic stimulation she had to rely on mushrooms; which were plentiful, but by no means uniformly "magical." This meant many backbreaking searches on hands and knees for Buffy, and they were very seldom rewarded. She had found and licked a toad once, but that, too, was a disappointment. She had sworn off toads after that and would never talk about the practice again.

It was getting late. Senga would have a headache in the morning. Maybe not if she puked tonight. She scowled at Buffy. With her one good eye, her scowl was quite formidable.

"Who told you that?"

Owl-like, Buffy turned her entire head to look at Senga. "Told me what?" she blinked.

Senga reached for the pipe. "The thing about the Abbess and the Guatemanian!" She clenched the pipe between her teeth, and Buffy fell to one side, laughing. A small pig ran out of her ear. Senga scowled.

"What's so funny?"

Buffy was holding herself around the middle and weeping with laughter so hard she could barely choke out, "You look like Popeye, man!"

Senga stood up quickly, banging her head on the low ceiling of Buffy's shelter. She took the pipe out from between her teeth and threw it at Buffy. "I'm outta here," she said, and left. And left. And then she left.

The moon on the water of the inlet, where Buffy obtained the water for her still, was bright, waxing gibbous; it would be full in a day or two. Senga shielded her eyes. Before they had gone their separate ways the women had agreed to gather at the clearing next to the Carousel at the next full moon; that could be tomorrow. Who knew? Senga's head already hurt. She would try to make it home tonight, and sleep until it was time to prepare for the Gathering.

And she did make it back to her shelter, and she did sleep a sleep of sorts. She slept long and fitfully and deep, and came to with a throat like scorched sand and a volcanic, bilious thirst—no wonder; she was soaked in both sweat and piss. Her head was filled with glass shards that were trying to work their way out through her eyeballs, and no matter how still she tried to hold her head and no matter in which direction she laid it, her surroundings responded by whirling violently in the opposite direction before slowly swinging to a stop, whereupon the contents of her stomach emptied themselves, again, and again, until her stomach itself threatened to give itself up and walk out of her body with its hands up. Losing consciousness was a mercy when it finally happened, and of how many times it happened before she finally recovered her senses she had no notion. She regained and lost consciousness again and again, and passed some hours when she shook until she couldn't remember ever not shaking. She tried to force her legs to carry her to the stream for water but they only laughed and then gave up. A chilly sheen of sweat glossed her skin, and caused her to shiver with cold, although the night was mild. She could feel her bones, cold as iron, but soft as jelly, and when the shaking stopped, the jerks began. Voluptuous waves that felt like imminent death and precarious life chased each other across her body and mind, until she knew no more and subsided into a tremulous silence.

* * *

The Abbess orgasmed delicately, a gentle tensing of muscles telling her partner to stop. She required only infrequent servicing—this time it had been Hagar's turn. Hagar, who had been an indifferent lover in the Big World

78

before the Crash, paid close attention to the Abbess's likes and dislikes now; there was no better way to curry favor, in this or any other world, than by being the purveyor of pleasure. She serviced other women and they serviced her, and the Abbess had others as well, but Hagar was best.

Hagar got to her feet and pretended to look at the hourglass. Surreptitiously, she rubbed her jaw. If the Abbess had a weakness, it was that she tended to be sensitive to criticism, so much so that she saw reproaches where none were intended; nevertheless, Hagar's jaw was sore. She forced herself to smile and then turned to face the Abbess. "I'm getting some water. Do you want some?" The Abbess reclined onto her upstretched arms and nodded, yawning like a cat. Hagar left the tented pavilion inside the Carousel where the Abbess slept, in order to fetch the water.

The Abbess, Abigail/Avigail Rivka Bronfman Barrow Renton that-had-been, watched her friend's retreating form and sat up languidly. Outside, the women were preparing for the Full of the Moon Gathering. They pulled rude wooden benches they'd hacked from the forest trees into the clearing, and covered the dais where the Abbess and Hagar would preside over the evening's events, seated upon tree-stump furniture before a painted birchbark screen. The Abbess listened to the familiar preparations. It had now been some months since the very first Full Moon Gathering, when the women had written The Rules.

There had been firelight, then, and a thrill in the air, as by this time they knew they were castaways, shipwrecked in an arboreal ocean by what means and for what purpose they knew not; all they knew was that they were alive, and those left alive now intended to go on living. It would be the purpose of this gathering to determine how.

Thirty or so women and girls had gathered in what had turned out to be a parking lot that had been built to accommodate visitors to the Carousel in the park—the women had figured out that much; the buses had been traveling along the winding city road that had the unlikely name of Forest Parkway when whatever it was that had happened, had happened. Some said earthquake, some said asteroid strike, some said the end of the world. Senga had thought the first scenario the most likely, and in this she was close to the truth—not that it really mattered.

By the time of that first Moon Meeting, when the women had lit torches and burned rubbish in metal barrels, a hierarchy had begun to emerge; a social order, and, more importantly, a mythos. The Abbess had taken charge, of course, aided by Hagar and her Acolytes, and by the time Senga arrived at the meeting, some things had already been decided.

* * *

Hagar returned with the water, which the Abbess accepted wordlessly. Hagar backed out of the sleep-chamber gingerly; she had work to do, but she needn't have bothered with deference. The Abbess was indifferent to her now, lost in memory of the first Moon Meeting.

* * *

Thirty women and girls had turned dirty faces to the firelight, and the Abbess stood before them on a concrete slab that was inlaid with alternating squares of dark and light stone; a concrete chessboard in what had been a public park. Senga, late to the meeting, smiled with closed lips. She kept to herself on the outmost fringe of the group, barely within the circle of firelight. She crossed her arms over her chest, and watched. She had been slender and strong in those days, and her hair had only begun to go grey since the crash; it still stood out from her head stiffly, falling in wiry auburn waves to below the bottom of her shoulder blades.

The air beyond the firelight's reach was turning chill in the blue light of the full moon; some of the smaller girls shivered, and a few were crying. All were hungry. The old concrete chess table on which the Abbess now stood, Senga observed, was matched by two others, and at those two—flanking the Abbess—Hagar and Buffy sat. Hagar had a pot of what looked, from where Senga was standing, like red paint. Buffy, Senga now saw, had lugged a plank of wood the width of a barn door to the makeshift stage; she had tried, mostly unsuccessfully, to cover it with a blanket recovered from the riding stables nearby; so Buffy's been scavenging, too, thought Senga. Her head hurt.

Buffy pulled the blanket off now, and steadied the edge of the wood planking on the chess table nearest her. Standing on the middle chess table, the Abbess was in full voice, and she cried, "Behold; the Rules of the Forest," and to Senga's mild disgust, as the blanket was tugged off, there were several crudely painted sentences to be seen on the board, red paint smears running and blobbing down the wood, but legible, if she squinted. Two of the Abbess's Acolytes were dispatched to help steady the planking; a night breeze was rising and ruffling the forest leaves. It had seemed to Senga that they were whispering, millions of whispers behind millions of leafy hands.

The Abbess's voice was joined by Buffy's and Hagar's, and the voices of the thirty or so women and girls gradually joined in. All except Senga, who was too bewildered and appalled to understand what was happening, and, in truth, a bit suspicious, too, as if this were all a joke the others were playing on her. The women chanted the words they read:

The Rules of the Forest:
1. **All women are created equal, and are as sisters.**
2. **No woman shall deny, discourage, or shame another woman, or prevent her from expressing her innermost self.**
3. **No woman shall strike another woman.**

4. **The Forest giveth, and the Forest taketh away.**

5. **All men are beasts.**

6. **You shall not suffer a man to live in the Forest proper, except when as needed for the Snatch. The Rules of the Snatch are Three:**
   - **Catch them.**
   - **Ride them.**
   - **Kill them.**

Upon reading these last three words, Senga was disquieted. *Catch whom, exactly?* But before she could consider this question further, she was nonplussed as Buffy passed the steadying of the Rules Board off to the Acolytes, entirely, with an elaborate flourish. She stepped forward, cleared her throat, and, to Senga's ongoing surprise, produced from one of her numerous pockets an undamaged pitch pipe. Flamboyantly, and with tremendous gravitas, she blew a note, and began to sing, to a tune that reminded Senga of either "Blueberry Hill" or "La Bamba:"

It's catch, before kill,

Cause a girl needs a thrill,

We must get our fill,

And don't let any spill!

As Buffy, bowing deeply, swept the tabletop with her mouse-colored hair, the women and girls clapped and cheered. The ones who had been crying were now wiping away their tears, smiling and hugging one another, and the Abbess was hugging Buffy, who went back to holding the Rules Board along with the Acolytes, a shy and humble smile illuminating her plain, broad face. Senga had a brief spasm of uncertainty; this was a joke, right? What were they singing about? Why were they cheering?

The brief spasm turned to profound confusion. In all Senga's wanderings she had searched, every sense on alert, for a sign that the forest contained anyone other than herself and the other women who had been on the buses, and found nothing. Yet these women were talking as if there were an invisible population of men in the forest who *might* just be listening. And they were talking utter nonsense. Senga shook her head. Nothing about this made sense.

The Abbess turned to face Hagar, and although Senga knew the Abbess couldn't see her as long as she stayed out of the firelight, it seemed to Senga that her enemy stared at her for the briefest of seconds before addressing the crowd. Without realizing it, Senga had put her hand to her chin and seemed about to swallow her fingers. With the other hand she rubbed her head and began to back away further from the firelight's glare, all the while staring in astonishment at the admittedly paltry and makeshift, yet somehow *because* of that, sadly powerful spectacle. *How long was I out?* She caught herself as she stumbled back against a shaggy oak, and heard more:

"Women of the Woods, we are here tonight by the will of the Heavenly Mother, who has preserved us and protected

84

us and will never forsake us as long as we obey these rules and any others that the group may deem necessary in future to worship her properly and guard ourselves from the depredations of men, at whose hands we have suffered so much!" There was cheering at this last bit, although some of the smaller girls were yawning, and one was picking her nose. The nearest grown woman slapped the child's hand away from her face and made a disgusted noise. As soon as the woman's back was to the child again, the little girl shrugged and resumed her olfactory excavations.

At the front of the crowd, the Abbess scanned the darkening perimeter of the woods and went on, her rich contralto voice portentious, admonitory: "Any man left alive who hears my voice, pay heed. The tables are turned. If you dare breach our defenses, we will use you up and then rid ourselves of you. We will not go back to the way things were." Women and girls shouted approval, and some shook what Senga had taken for walking sticks, but now realized might be spears. The Abbess continued, this time addressing the gathered women.

"We are not men, we do not decree and levy, but we confer and come to consensus. We now invite you to come to the board, take up the paintbrush, and write what rules seem good to you—ask your heavenly Mother for guidance, and it will come." The Abbess opened her arms wide, and a thin trickle of women and girls made its way up to the board. *This must have been planned—no way would she waste the paint letting anybody write whatever they wanted,* thought Senga, crouching down further away from the firelight, in the lee of the shaggy elm. Up front, obscured by the orange flames, a thin, lovely woman with golden skin that shone in the firelight, and crisp, ink-black hair had hold of the paintbrush in the long fingers of her left hand and was already writing. When she was finished, she stood aside to let the others read:

No woman shall call another woman a bitch,

And as she finished the final, predictable word, a shout went up, and then another, and the women were calling out more words, and the Abbess was nodding, and so the golden-skinned woman painted all the words the women called out, until the list read:

No woman shall call another woman a bitch,

or a cunt,

or a whore,

or a slag,

or a tramp,

or a couze,

or a slut,

or a slapper, a banger, a hole or a twat, etc.

No Woman shall own another Woman.

No Woman shall have a secret from the group.

Every Woman shall benefit from the labor of the group.

Private property is crime.

No football.

Then Hagar and Buffy disappeared behind the concrete chessboard-stage, and the Acolytes followed them. The Abbess was standing above the crowd, absurdly balanced on her tiny, concrete chessboard "stage," and, holding both arms outstretched, she turned her hands palmside down, patting the air above the women's heads and making shushing noises, which the women and girls gradually obeyed.

"Sit, please," the Abbess repeated until all the women but Senga, who was still hidden behind her tree, were seated. The ground was hard-packed dirt here on the rim of the old parking lot, and the grass was sparse. Exhaust fumes from the automobiles of hundreds of long-ago visitors to the Carousel had coated the spiky grass blades with a seemingly permanent layer of soot and grime. That was when Senga noticed what the Abbess was wearing—at the moment when the women and girls, instructed to sit cross-legged, bare-legged, on the hard-packed and grimy ground, pulled their flimsy, worn-out skirts around their legs for what protection from the dirt and cold they could afford—Senga noticed that the Abbess was wearing a . . . there was no other word for it . . . it was a *habit.* The Abbess had gotten herself a nun's habit.

Oh, there was no wide black leather belt from which a rosary could hang, but the layered cut of the thing, the heavy white lawn fabric from which it was fashioned, and above all, the binding headdress and furled black bombazine veil were both unmistakably home-made and equally unmistakably an approximation of a nun's floor-sweeping habit. From her hiding place behind the shaggy elm, Senga ventured a grim little smile. She hadn't noticed that it was a habit, and might not have noticed for a long while, were it not for the extremely nun-like way the Abbess swept the folds of her heavy, white lawn skirt away from the ground, and with what disdain she pinched the fabric between forefinger and thumb to lift it away from the earth, daintily (but modestly, so that no excess of flesh would show). Senga smiled more grimly. *Trust **her**.*

Evidently the evening's festivities were only beginning. Once the women and girls were seated on the forest floor, the Abbess clapped her hands, and from the darker-than-dark aperture that led into the Carousel, Hagar and Buffy re-emerged, followed by the nameless Acolytes, who carried between them a huge, cylindrical metal barrel from which steam was rising; there was a pair of holes near the top rim, and opposite them another pair of holes. Through these, rough poles, stripped branches, likely, had been forced, so that the Acolytes could walk, each resting a pole on either shoulder, one in front of the other, so that the metal barrel was suspended between them. The barrel looked heavy, and it was evidently very hot, from the care the Acolytes took not to touch it or to let it touch their bare skin. Senga watched in silent amazement. *How long* was *I out*? she wondered, and rubbed her forehead.

The Acolytes put the drum down in front of the Abbess. A murmur went up from the assembled women, which the Abbess did nothing to quell. Senga watched and waited.

Finally, the Abbess spoke. "Sisters," she said, "come and eat." Hagar murmured something to her and she added, "One at a time, of course. Form a line here. Hagar and Buffy will give you each a bowl, and Renee and Alice (she indicated the Acolytes) will fill it for you. There is enough for all." And so the women and girls lined up, and as Senga bleakly observed, there was no thought to feeding the young ones first, or if there were, it was quickly submerged in the demanding hunger of those older and stronger. Senga felt herself a little sick. Some kind of stew was being doled out, into bowls and cups and old tin cans, discarded bottles and small tubs the women and girls had scavenged. Senga sniffed; there was *meat* in the stew.

Looking around, she started counting . . . one, two, three…oh, she couldn't remember how many of them there had been on the buses, and how many had died at first, but she hoped, she hoped, that whoever it was they were eating had died naturally, as the other possibility was too horrible to imagine.

But imagine it she had, and the vision in her mind sent her flailing backwards and crashing into the bracken, which is where the others found her; sprawled in a bush, her legs splayed and her arms caught by bare branches. There was a scuffle and a clamor that came from what had been the front of the group, where the Abbess was, and Senga heard the Abbess's voice clang, "Bring a torch!"

To her surprise, she found herself pinned in the synthetic yellow beam emanating from the lens of an ordinary, two-cell, grey metal flashlight with a red plastic top; it had been in the driver's toolbox and it was wielded by the Acolyte Alice, now, in two shaking hands. Out of the darkness between the fire and the flashlight's beam walked the Abbess; approaching Senga, she reached out her hand. Senga grabbed it and the Abbess pulled her out of the bush. Senga did not thank her.

"Nice of you to join us, Senga. We were about to form a search party."

"I'll bet," said Senga, playing for time. Her head throbbed and her stomach was threatening to empty itself on the ground at her feet; or it would have if it hadn't already been emptied, violently, earlier. She brushed down her clothes; unlike the Abbess, she had no special raiment and was feeling somewhat chilled as well as embarassed. The Abbess, reveling in her enemy's discomfort, smirked. "Poor Senga . . . always . . . underdressed." She turned on her heel and signaled Alice to extinguish the torch. "Save the batteries."

"Always late to the party, too," added Hagar, who had trotted up just as Senga was being rescued from the bush. Then she turned to follow the Abbess.

Buffy, still and slow, stared at Senga across the darkening clearing and shrugged. She put up her hand with the index and middle fingers in the shape of the letter V, then she turned and lumbered across the grass, into the darker darkness of the Carousel, and joined the others who were already gathered inside   with   their   spoons   and   bowls.

CHAPTER NINE
SENGA ALONE

THAT HAD BEEN LONG AGO, AND SENGA HAD LEARNED NOT TO eat or drink or smoke anything from Buffy's hands anymore, although she still visited Buffy on occasion in her redoubt, that clearing in the center of a stand of Silver Maples close to the water's edge, to which Buffy had added over time, binding and winding, shoring and reinforcing, enhancing and embellishing. Her pot plantation was thriving, and if she had never managed to synthesize LSD, she still made and drank her fierce *poteen*-like brew and her diet never suffered for lack of protein.

Buffy, like most of the other women, had found her niche. She'd taught herself butchery, practicing on small things at first, and her friends, the stoners, she taught to cut too, in exchange for keeping them in weed. The trapping and killing she did herself, though.

Hagar continued her interrupted teaching career, and if she was now only a teacher from necessity, truly, she was gifted with the malignant pettiness and aimless cruelty to have been a qualified teacher of the type she and Buffy and Senga would have suffered in the Big World of the Time Before. She had a natural gift.

The Abbess kept the rules and the ceremonies, the calendar and the rituals. She lived in the Carousel with her Acolytes, and took no part in the everyday work of maintaining the world in the woods. That left Senga.

After that first Moon Meeting, Senga had begun to walk. She walked in the direction she thought would lead her out of the forest, but the forest was tricky; the forest was alive. It had its own purposes and its own rules, purposes and rules the women knew not.

Senga had been wrong about some things that long ago night when she and the Abbess had argued: Live or Die. *I'm not the suicide type,* she had discovered. But she wasn't the type to fall in line behind the Abbess, either, and so she began to walk, as if she could walk her way home, out of the forest and back to a world that didn't exist any more, except in her memory.

In that memory, as she walked, Senga visited and revisited all the places and people she knew she would never see again; her mother and father, her siblings, the friends and neighbors all around them in their old, once-grand, lately shabby, apartment building on Parsons Boulevard, the boys and men she had known, the rivalrous women and girls she had played with but from whom she was beginning to drift away. She had these images for company now, and they were to be all she *would* have, until Pink would come to her, sometime in the unseen future. The Women of the Woods had convinced themselves that they were alone in the world, but Senga was more alone, still, and she felt it, keenly. She felt lost, isolated, and abandoned. The walking was automatic, and witless, but it was also her hope.

She walked through days and nights until one morning after sunup she could no longer place one foot in front of the other, and there it was that she collapsed in exhaustion and despair. When she rallied, she looked around and saw that the forest here was less wild, the terrain more level; there was water nearby—she could hear it. The trees didn't grow so thickly together, and there was a semicircular clearing around which a thin grove of birches stood at attention. She would build her first home here. As she assessed the possibilities of this bit of earth, out of the corner of her eye, she saw a bright shape in the air that moved, then darted forward, then hung low in the sky, *so* still except for its wings, which beat so fast they blurred as they held its tiny body in suspension. *My first hummingbird,* Senga thought, and smiled to herself, a wan and listless little smile before the enormity of her isolation and forsakenness crashed in on her. Then she wept, great convulsive tears, with loud wailings and shuddering yawps as she gulped in air. How long that lasted she couldn't know, but since she had decided she was not the suicide type, she gradually pushed herself to her feet, and headed toward the sound of running water; she would have to pull herself together and set about the business of surviving.

So that's what she did—that first afternoon once she'd cried herself out and had several gulps of cold water, she'd crawled into the birch clearing and slept on the bare ground; but she was so weary she wouldn't have noticed if there had been a bed of gravel under those trees. When she awoke, for the first time since the crash, she awoke on her back, looking up through birch branches at the same blue sky she had known forever; there were even white clouds being blown across the small, naked patch of azure heaven. Senga got to her knees and prayed. "If you are there, protect me. If you are there, show me the way home." That was all. As she placed her hands on either side of her knees to help her stand, she noticed the faint sheen of moss on the spot where she had slept, which had been bare and brown the night before.

Those first days in her glade were a jumble of problems to be solved, and priorities to be made. Did she want to eat? She'd have to find something to eat, or pick it, or kill it. The last idea held no appeal for Senga. Although she had been a voracious consumer of cheeseburgers wrapped in foil and the kind of fried chicken that came in a red and white-striped cardboard bucket with a picture of a bloated, goateed, and bespectacled southern gent on the outside, she had no stomach for catching, much less killing, her own food. But she was hungry, and her belly was making twisting, growling sounds. She had long ago finished the snacks she'd brought with her for the march, and she'd gone through her share of the common food the women had gathered from the buses and divided among themselves. She remembered something she had read and as she remembered it, she said it aloud, as persons who live alone often do. So began Senga's habit of talking to herself. *A person can survive three minutes without air, three days without water, three weeks without food; okay. So I've got the air and the water. I need food.*

She looked around, as if she expected to find a supermarket, or at least an apple tree, on the spot. Her looking did have one good result; she began to remember this part of the forest now, or she thought she remembered being here before. It had changed, and would change more, but there was a ridge directly in front of her that she had seen before. She made her way up the slope toward that ridge that looked familiar, marked with a large, long-dead oak tree that had fallen against another instead of falling all the way to the ground, a bit of luck, since if it had fallen it would have been covered with leaves, sprouted mushrooms, and rotted away; instead it had remained where it fell for many years, from the

96

time Senga had made love with her young man near the stables, and it was here still, as a signpost. And if *it* was here, the wild strawberries might also be here. And they were.

Of course Senga gorged on them, and was almost sick. But she was careful not to eat them all, before wiping her mouth with her hands and heading back to the birch grove and its nearby stream. As she dipped her head down to the water and drank, some impulse made her pause and say "Thanks." As she did, an errant gust of wind blew across the forest floor and lifted twigs and branches in a leafy sussuration that Senga took for a benediction.

CHAPTER TEN

THE LIFE OF THE FOREST

THE FOREST WAS ALIVE. NOT SOLELY IN THE USUAL WAY that forests, and grasslands, deserts, and moors, bogs, and savannahs, and marshes, and swamps are alive; no. The forest had *intentionality,* it had will. If it didn't give sustenance to the women and girls in quite the way the Abbess had predicted, still, it gave to them, not always what they wanted, but most assuredly what they needed.

It began to seem to Senga that the forest had a "soul" that needed expression, or that it had an idea of what it wanted to be that it was impatient to realize. Time after time, in the early days, Senga's younger self had watched, goggle-eyed, the unnaturally rapid growth of certain stands of trees, with an attendant squealing and squeaking as the bark tried to outpace the burgeoning, pulpy wood inside. Birches and maples she had seen growing like bamboo, shooting measurably taller (and rounder) in hours instead of years. The process worked in reverse, as well, and Senga had rubbed her eyes in the beginning, but then become almost jaded by viewing the compressed disintegration of copses and groves, and easily familiar with the almost inaudible whispers they made in their dying.

Of course, on the day Senga and Hagar would challenge each other at Kettledrum Hill, the pace of the forest's changing had long-since slowed. No longer did meadows flower, outbuildings collapse, or new groves appear overnight, nor did the earth buckle up as if bored by giant moles making giant tunnels in the space of an afternoon, but the rhythm of growth, although it had slowed, had never stopped altogether. After her initial shock, Senga had been reminded of the thing called "television," and of sitting on the floor in her parents' house and watching the images that emanated from its glowing, glaucous eye on a Sunday evening—watching something, Senga remembered, called "The Wonderful World of Disney." This program often presented images of the natural world—entire life cycles of plants compressed into minutes, frog spawn erupting into frog in the blink of an eye, a moon that traversed the crisp, inky dome of the night in a trice, all while a deep, fatherly voice explained . . . something. "Magic," young Senga had called it.

She had liked television, even the programs like *Combat,* which was about soldiers and war, and which her brother had insisted they watch. Or wrestling, which was stupid, and ugly, and clearly fake, but to which her old aunt Tee-anna had been devoted. Tee-anna had died long before Senga got on the bus that last day, but Senga's brother, by then almost grown-up and just a year younger than she, had been alive, although they had not seen each other in some time. She wondered, in those early days, if she ever would see him, or anyone from the World Before, again.

It occupied her mind, this wondering, as she wandered like Alice, through a ceaselessly changing, now-you-see-it, now-you-don't landscape. Thinking of the people and the things she had known, and wondering if she would know them again. There was in Senga a strange and placid acceptance, a fatalism wedded to an indomitable resolve, which allowed her to bear the otherwise unbearable.

While Hagar and the Abbess were power-seekers, and Buffy sought oblivion and bliss, Senga was driven by an inner conviction that things could and should make sense, and that she could affect the outcome of events. *I can't do everything*, she thought. *But I can do something.* Senga had intelligence, a practical, optimistic nature, a bold curiosity, an uncrushable spirit, and a great deal of common sense.

As she wandered, she began to be aware of the will of the forest, where it wanted to wilden and where it wanted to tame. She followed the taming impulse as it beat down bracken and gorse and made paths, always leading her deeper into the heart of itself, away from the others. One day, it would lead her to the half-buried Fire Relay Station. But in the early years, she always circled back in her wanderings, as she told herself "to keep an eye on" the others. Hagar and the Abbess she distrusted, and Buffy filled her with despair, but she was not the suicide type, as she knew well, and she needed contact with something more human than the intentionality she sensed in the forest. The man she had loved once had called the thing that Senga needed "a God with some skin on Him," and she'd understood—he'd meant people.

Buffy was brutish, and ugly and only semi-conscious the majority of the time, but she was human, a person—almost too much so. And so, every month, it seemed that the forest sensed Senga's need for her own kind, and it led her back, at the full of the moon, to her first small hut in the clearing not far from the Carousel and the others, the place where she could see and not be seen by them, the place where, in the future, she would meet her foster-daughter, Pink.

Living so much inside her mind, Senga didn't notice the exact moment when her memories, her imaginings, her wishes and her dreams collapsed in on each other, and coalesced, but there came a day when she began to feel she had come loose from time. Often she'd thought, in the beginning, upon awakening, "I'll go to so-and-so's house today," or "I wonder what's at the movies." Then she would gasp as she realized that she was cut off from old friends, and movies, and her brother, and her parents, and the man she had loved, and her entire life. As the years would pass, these losses would be less keenly felt, less like a knife-wound, more like a bone-deep bruise.

CHAPTER ELEVEN

DREAMING AND WAKING

IKE EVERY RITUAL THAT EVER WAS, THE SNATCH was the reenactment of a myth. Like every myth, the myth of the Snatch was a mixture of, fact and fiction, lies and truth, all in service of a truth that was truer than true. And as happens with all rituals, when the deep truth of the Snatch began to be forgotten, the forms of the ritual became more rigid, and adherence to them more strenuously defended.

Senga had observed these principles at work in her own long-ago girlhood. Sunday attendance at the ritual called the Sacrifice of the Mass was obligatory—Senga and her classmates had fidgeted on the narrow, wooden "kneelers" under a soaring gothic vault, while on the altar the priest turned water into wine, and the roll was taken by the pickle-faced, sad young nuns who were, during the rest of the week, their schoolteachers. On Monday mornings, retribution was extracted from those who had displayed an insufficiency of piety, or worse, "missed Mass" altogether. (Public shaming for the children who were easily cowed, corporal punishment for the bold, all backed up with the promise of hellfire unless amends were made in the Confessional box.) Senga shuddered when she remembered how she had feared the sleepy old priests behind the curtains and the screens, and the snappish nuns—she had experienced it all, and she remembered. When she first observed the nascent, horrid thing that was to become the Snatch, she knew, she thought to herself, this is what one Mary knew in Bethlehem, and another learned on Golgotha. It may have been what Eve knew in the garden, as well. *This is how gods are born, and myths are made, and the wildness of human hearts is beaten down and held in check.*

Senga would observe the Snatch, but from a distance. After that first time, she never took part. Aside from the rape of the half-dead driver, she knew she would have no more to do with men, unless it was in her dreams. She dreamed often of men; of her father, with his tough pink skin; of her brother, younger, and weaker, and handsome, and easily hurt. She dreamt of their old doctor, who had sewn her eyebrow back together when her brother, growth spurt begun and done, had outgrown her temper and her bossiness. She dreamt of boys from college—fumbling youths, all mouth and teeth and tongue, and she dreamt of their rough, eager sex—straining and ready to surge, and hard, and hot, and tight inside their dungarees as they clashed against her in stairwells, or doorways, or in borrowed cars. Of the man she had once loved, she rarely dreamed. Except once.

She had been dreaming of him the morning she heard the voices. Real voices, not ones inside her head.

She had slept that night in the soft, mossy clearing near the stream where the strawberries grew, the stream that splashed along for a while before disappearing into a natural declivity under a recent, but very solid-looking rockfall, close by the spot where she'd made her bed. Senga was, she now saw, as she looked around for the source of the sound, near the base of a sort of cliff, composed of fallen rocks, and, further up, a band of dark soil which supported the growth of what looked like an ordinary, if somewhat taller than normal, boxwood hedge, with innumerable shiny, spear-shaped leaves growing in all directions. The hedge—as she could see by standing on tiptoe and peering between the branches of the trees around her moss-bed—extended above the tops of the taller trees in this part of the woods; it seemed that its roots grew in a layer of soil at a level with the treetop canopy. Senga's clearing was, therefore, at the bottom of a sort of cliff, in a fairytale spot, really. If the other women could see how well she had fared! They probably thought she'd have crawled back to them by now. They were probably starving and killing each other for the crumbs in the seams of their knapsacks! Senga compressed her lips and exhaled through her nose in satisfaction. She was doing well. Things were looking up.

The air in this part of the forest was populated with small white butterflies attracted by the pink and white clover nearby, and the place was loud with bees and iridescent with dragonflies, and she would have made it her permanent camp, if not for what happened there that morning.

It was men's voices she'd heard, calling her out of her sleep.

"Fuck! Jesus fuck!"

"You asshole, Frank—you're gonna get us killed!"

Senga bolted upright, and the hair on her arms stood erect, and her mouth fell open. Silence.

She *had* heard it, she had. It hadn't been part of her dream. She looked around wildly, whipping her head from side to side—her injured eye was healing slowly and she would eventually lose the use of it, but she didn't know that on this day of the men's voices. The rapid movement of hear head made her eye throb; but she ignored the pain and crouched to make herself small as she tried to determine which direction the unmistakably male, unmistakably real voices were coming from. Then she heard them again.

"It was here, I told ya!"

"Well it ain't here no more . . . I shoulda known better than to listen to you . . . fucking idiot!"

High above the rockfall, behind the hedge, Senga realized, with a burst of joy—that's where the voices were coming from. She looked around, but she had nothing she could bring back to the others, nothing that would permit her to say, "See—we are not alone—there are others!" It didn't occur to her that the Abbess and Hagar and Buffy didn't share her feelings; didn't want to be discovered, nor to discover that there were others outside the woods. She was blind to the danger she was in, both from the unseen voices and from the other women, but she was bursting with excitement and it overran her caution, and she called out: "Hello!"

High up, behind the hedge, the deeper of the voices yelled,

"Shut up, you jackass! I heard something!"

"It's an echo," said the higher voice.

"If it was an echo, it would've said 'fucking idiot'!" said Deeper Voice. "Where are you?" it called. For the briefest of moments, Senga considered that she had no point of reference, and so no possible way to tell the men (and she was certain now that they were men, although not yet how many) where she was, before crying, "I'm here—down here— on the other side of the—bushes—be careful, there's rocks, and a cliff . . . I'm at the bottom . . .".

"Hold on," said Deeper Voice, and there was a sound of yells and scuffling as he and the other argued some more, an argument Deeper Voice evidently won, and by the time the men had finished, Senga had clambered half-way up the rock face, following the sounds of their voices. She heard hacking and tearing above her, too, as the men attempted to break through the hedge, which, she now realized, might be more like a gigantic, wild, flat shrubbery than the tame and logical thing Senga had called a "hedge" in her life in the Big World before the buses crashed. It could be terribly thick up there; it might take them a while to break through. She looked around. From the bottom of the hedge to the forest floor, she estimated was a twenty-foot drop. Manageable, if expected, but a potential leg- or neck-breaker if not. "I'm below you," she cried, when suddenly one, and then the second, crashed through the roots and fell speeding past her where she clung to the rocks. They fell fast, propelled into thin air by the impetus of their own eagerness and the strength of their own arms, and the persecond persecond force of gravity, which had not changed.

Senga climbed down from her perch slowly; she was shaking in all her limbs. She reached the bottom of the rocky cliff and stopped, suddenly wary. Winded and shocked, the men were struggling to stand up, only yards away from her. A lone bee swam in front of Senga's face, and she swatted it away.

Slowly, slowly, the young men regained their footing. They bent over, hands on knees, to recover their breathing, and when they did, they grinned toothy grins at each other. Success.

"Holy shit!" said the first to recover his breath. "You were right . . . ."

Deeper Voice took longer to recover, but when he did, he looked directly at Senga. He pointed her out to his companion with an elbow jab and an index finger. The grins were turned on her now.

She froze, gripped by a sudden terror that held her rooted for long, slow-moving seconds. A moment before there had been only a frenzy of joyous hope, but something in the way the two men looked at her turned her guts to ice.

They were not prepossessing—whatever the hardship that the cataclysm had wrought on the women in the woods, it seemed to have been matched in the world outside. Senga couldn't know this, or know that she was looking at a mirror image of herself—only one that possessed a Y chromosome. The men were filthy, and hunger-thinned, and they stank; she could smell them from yards away. (Of course, they could also smell her.) The one nearer to her, the one with the higher voice, was the more slightly built of the pair—the hair on his head was the color of putty, or would have been if it hadn't been so filthy. The men's exertions had brought the sweat out on their foreheads, and it dripped from their brows and made their already threadbare shirts cling to their skin. Senga could almost count their ribs. She could hear, if not feel, their breath. It had the metallic smell of starvation. And although they were clearly suffering hunger, as she had been, they were still men—bigger, stronger, tougher. The smell of them stood in her nostrils, and raised the hair on her arms, and she panicked. She ran.

Blindly and in terror, she ran toward the others; or toward where she thought the others had been when she saw them last. She crashed through the undergrowth and the men crashed through behind her, shouting at her, calling her names.

"Crazy bitch!"

"Come back, you fucking cunt!"

But she wouldn't and couldn't stop—her blood was pounding in her ears, and her eyes stung as sweat mixed with her tears and blinded her. In her unseeing terror, she ripped wildly at vines, unheeding, even as they snapped back and tore her skin. Her one grace was that she knew the forest, and her pursuers did not.

But that advantage couldn't last long. Though she was goaded by dread and spurred by the will to survive, her pursuers were stronger, and could run faster. Stinging nettles whipped her bare legs, and her breath scratched and caught in her chest, and she knew she couldn't go one more step, when she heard a bigger crash amidst all the crashing behind her, and the screams of the men changed. There was still rage, and there were curses, but there was also now pain. Senga—too far gone to detect that note of agony in the men's voices—gave herself up for dead, and closed her eyes, waiting for the bone-breaking welter of blows and the ripping of hair she was sure would come, but she waited in vain. Although she could still hear them, her pursuers had suddenly disappeared from sight.

From where she lay panting on the forest floor, she raised her head to look around. Another moment, she saw, as her vision cleared, and she would have reached her goal— Buffy's pot plantation was staked out directly in her path, and Buffy—maybe in response to the men's screams—was lumbering out of her shelter, pulling up the straps of her ubiquitous farmer's overalls, and scratching herself. Senga began to shudder and laugh with relief as she lay in a heap on the ground, and Buffy approached.

"Wow," she said. "What happened to you?"

Buffy's manner was nonplussed, as if it were nothing, as if she saw Senga, raw and panicked, every day, and collapsed on the forest floor in a quivering, fear-struck heap— or as if she were seeing her as she might have in the old days, on a city street, when Senga had been caught in the rain without an umbrella. But what was astonishing to Senga was that Buffy seemed to be *expecting* her, or at least to be expecting *someone*.

Buffy lumbered through the screen of saplings that separated her from her old friend, and paused to pull Senga to her feet before striding on to where the men's screams were loudest. She looked down, then turned a toothy grin to Senga. "Got'em."

Where she had them, Senga, approaching, now saw, was in a hole in the ground that had been covered over with leaves; a trap. Buffy's face was split by her smile—it was almost painful for Senga to look at. *Is she actually drooling?*

"Luna was stealing my shit," she explained, unhelpfully, but Senga understood; Buffy had dug the pit to catch her. "Um," Buffy puzzled, looking down at her catch. "Those are *guys*."

Warily, Senga shook her head. "Yes . . . " she said. "Those are guys." She hooted and slapped Buffy on the back. "You have an amazing grasp of the fucking obvious," she laughed. Imprecations and wordless screams came from the pit, and clods of earth flew out at the two women as well, as the men, enraged and in pain, began grabbing handsful of earth and hurling them up and out of the trap. Senga's high spirits were returning; *there are others, we're not alone, and I'm alive; I'm safe.* If these two were alive, maybe others were also; others who could be approached in the safety of numbers. A clod of earth with roots attached hit her on the forehead and broke apart; she wiped the crumbs off and grinned. *It could have been worse,* she smiled to herself, shaking her head. *It could have been me in the trap, or getting worked over by these two—*

"Why were you running?"

Senga made a wry face, and shrugged. "I panicked."

Buffy looked like she had heard the word "panic" before at some point during her life and was struggling to call up its meaning. She squinted at Senga.

"You stay here," she suggested, finally. "I'll go get the Abbess."

Fucking hell, thought Senga, *like I'm going to stay here and listen to this.* The men were making an awful racket; the fall had hardly been straight down, as Buffy's trap was not an engineered thing, not a well, but a lazy, badly made thing of equal parts expedience and inexperience. But Senga nodded, and Buffy turned to go.

Deeper Voice seemed to have landed unscathed, but Putty Hair was hurt; his reedy screams were painful to hear. Senga removed herself from earshot and waited to see what would happen when the Abbess arrived; she would enjoy sticking the pin into her little "World of Women" bubble! Senga's heart was still thudding, and her chest still hurt from the inside out. But she smiled. *Yes!* she thought, *I win! You won't be able to pretend we're alone now. You've got to admit there's something out there, other people, help . . . .* Relief washed over her, and a giddying sense of triumph. Senga plucked a blade of grass and drew it between her molars; she had found some long-forgotten beef jerky that had languished in her knapsack and eaten it last night. *Got it!* She had always taken care of her teeth. Among other things, once it seemed that they would live, Senga had begun to be concerned about how she and the other women would maintain their health if help never came, if they really were the only people left. Now that she knew they were not, she was reassured. She sucked her teeth. *It's better than nothing, but grass makes shitty dental floss.*

She lounged on the grass while she waited for Buffy to return with the Abbess. *There* are *others,* she told herself, smiling. *If the forest let them in, it might let us out. We can leave the forest. . . We're going home!* She cradled her head in her arms and dozed off. She slept that way for a while.

Chapter Twelve

Soap and Civilization

THEY ATE PUTTY HAIR FIRST.

T Senga was sitting cross-legged in the grass, recovering her wits and picking her teeth, when the Abbess marched up, flanked by two . . . archers. Senga thought she recognized Renee, but the other woman she couldn't name. Their kit was clearly hand-made and improvised, but there was no doubt; they were archers. The Abbess stepped, delicately and deliberately up to the very edge of the pit, and the screaming stopped briefly, as the men took hope of rescue. They didn't notice, but Senga did, the almost imperceptible signal to which the archers immediately responded. Before she could cry out, they had nocked their arrows and let fly, straight down into the pit. Putty Hair's final scream was a pitiable thing, less a scream, really, than a bubbling whine that trailed off into a gurgling whimper. He had screamed much louder on first breaking his leg upon falling into the trap. A curse from Deeper Voice rose out of the pit; followed by silence.

The Abbess turned to smile at Senga, whose mouth still formed the word "No," although she had made no sound. "A mercy, really," The Abbess smiled through closed lips, beatifically.

If Senga had thought herself beyond shock, she was to discover on this day that she was not. Rooted and frozen, she watched as the Abbess gave orders, and within minutes, she had instructed the archers to cover the remaining man in the pit, while Buffy came panting back along the path carrying a rusted, clanking pulley, followed by Luna, who carried an ordinary, wooden, carpenter's ladder, and Alice, who brought up the rear with a good length of stout hemp rope, the loose and dangling end of which threatened to trip her. *Everyone's been scavenging.*

As Senga watched, in dumb amaze, the women, directed with gestures and a few monosyllabic utterances by the Abbess, set the legs of the wide ladder astride the hole. Then Luna reached across and hooked the protesting pulley, through which Buffy had already threaded the rope, to the underside of the ladder's top step. They threw the rope down to the man who remained alive in the pit. The pulley squeaked. The Abbess stepped up to the edge of the pit, clearing her throat to command, "Tie it around him."

The man in the pit hesitated, and the archers nocked their bows. He began to comply. Putty Hair was a slippery, stiffening mess, but Buffy was, like her namesake, a beast of burden, and once the ropes were tight around the corpse, she made short work of pulling it out of the hole as the pulley shrieked and clanked.

The archers re-slung their bows onto their backs and helped wrestle the body across the lip of the hole and onto the grass. They humped and bumped him onto Buffy's shoulders, where he hung like a deer, dripping blood from his broken leg and his other wounds. Buffy set off down the path toward the Carousel, an archer on each side to prevent the blood-sodden mass that had been a man from slipping off her shoulders. The Abbess made to follow them, but turned to Senga.

"You are welcome to join us," she said, politely, as if she were speaking of tea and sandwiches, or even pizza. Senga looked toward the pit, so lately full of sound and fury and now so silent. The Abbess approached her. She wrinkled her nose, like a sweet child sharing a confidence, and tapped Senga on hers. "He'll keep." She waggled her fingers at the living man in the pit, and put her arm around Senga to lead her away from the death trap. "Sisters shouldn't be strangers," she crooned, only a whisper of reproach in her honeyed voice. Senga was too shocked; she gave no reply, but allowed the Abbess to lead her by the hand along the path toward the

Carousel. "We have much to do, and much to tell you." She continued to hold Senga's hand as her words wound around her like cords, slowly pulling her along the Abbess's path. Stray strands of hair had fallen across Senga's face; the Abbess smoothed them away tenderly, but her words were cold and direct: "You have much to tell us, too, don't you? Hhm." By way of reply Senga looked blankly at the Abbess and shuddered inwardly, but said nothing. The walk back to the Carousel was long, and Senga's steps were slow, somnambulant. But she allowed herself to be led by the hand like a child, as the Abbess pointed out various perfectly ordinary natural features as if they were recent discoveries, or exclaimed over some utterly pedestrian phenomenon, like a butterfly, or a bee. *How I hate her,* Senga was thinking, when suddenly, they were . . . *where?*

She saw now how the archers had been fetched so quickly; here (by the giant rhododendrons—she remembered *them*) the forest road curved, and suddenly there was a kind of encampment, or something between a bivouac and a garrison—at any rate it was an edifice, a rude fortification of wattle-and-daub. A frightened-looking pre-teen girl peered out of an opening in what Senga supposed was a wall, and greeted them with what could have been a salute, or just a tremulous wave. The Abbess accepted the salutation with another of her beatific nods. She and Senga continued to walk, past features Senga no longer quite recognized, and the Abbess kept up her bromidic monologue, eventually subsiding into a barely

117

audible humming that put Senga's teeth ever-so-slightly on edge.

And so in this way they continued, until they reached the vicinity of the Carousel, and still Senga recognized . . . nothing. How long ago had it been since she walked away? *A month, maybe. Maybe two.* She tried to calculate the number of meals she'd had; she had eked out the remaining bus rations as long as she could (including last night's beef jerky) and had lately been living off the strawberries and (more recently, spurred by hunger) some plants she recognized as milkweed and chicory. And of course she had been drinking from what she had begun to think of as "her" stream. The few nuts she had been able to extract from pine cones by snapping off the scales, as she had seen squirrels do, had hardly been worth the effort. She hadn't been wasting her energy, but she hadn't accomplished much, either. She had seen chipmunks and of course, tree squirrels, but had neither the heart nor the skill to catch and eat them. She had tried a worm, but couldn't bring herself to do more than put in her mouth and spit it right back out again. It *might* have been two months since she had walked away from the others. It *felt* like two months.

"Hi, Senga . . . "

"Hey!"

"What the . . ."

"How are you?"

"Where have *you* been?"

"We thought you were dead!"

118

These and other salutations rang out from women she hardly recognized and filled the air as the Abbess walked her across the wide, empty, recently-swept brown earthen patch that seemed to unroll like a tongue from the mouth of the Carousel. Around the periphery of the "tongue" were shelters, lean-tos, mostly, but Senga discerned a couple of crude tee-pees. Beyond and behind them stretched the darkening forest.

On the far side of the earth-and-patchy-grass field, partly concealed by the Carousel itself, was a scaffold or stage of some kind; there Buffy and the archers were doing something to the body of the man they had killed. These women had been busy, and Senga's face grew red, thinking of her own inactivity over the past few . . . she didn't even know how long. She remembered her inward gloating of just hours ago and her spirits sank.

The Abbess had led her to the entrance to the Carousel, which Senga now saw had been barricaded, and the barricade staffed by none other than Hagar. Suddenly Senga realized what was making the women so unrecognizable; they were *clean.* They were all dressed alike (except for Buffy, whose bib overalls seemed to have become a part of her body) and apart from Buffy, they were astonishingly *clean.*

"I love what you've done with the place," she jeered.

Hagar pushed aside the papers she had been pretending to do something with, looked up at the Abbess, then pinched her nose at Senga.

"Yes," said the Abbess, reading Hagar's unsubtle grimace and wiping her hands against each other as if to rid herself of filth, the hands with which she had lately so tenderly led Senga and touched her hair. "She needs a bath. See to it, Hagar. *I* need to lie down," the Abbess disappeared into the labyrinth of the Carousel's remodeled interior, momentarily parting a curtain that wafted toward Senga an aroma like frankincense as it fluttered closed behind her.

Hagar hauled herself out from behind her post and took Senga by the elbow, so that only the merest edges of her fingertips touched Senga's skin, as if she were poison. If Hagar had had a pair of tongs, she would have used them. "Come with me, and don't argue," she commanded.

"Who's arguing?" Senga allowed herself to be guided around to the back entrance of the Carousel, stumbling a little on the steps that she had forgotten were there, though she had walked them once or twice in her life before. Hagar sucked her teeth in impatience and pushed her harder.

"Just don't start. Tonight's an important night. I have . . . we all have a lot to prepare . . . we haven't all been rolling around like pigs in shit, like you have, from the look and the smell of you . . ."

"You haven't changed a bit," Senga was about to say, when she was brought up short alongside a dented metal wall, at least five feet tall and about eight feet long. It was the side of a rectangular, corrugated, metal . . . box, Senga supposed. Then she realized it was called a "dumpster," and that she had seen lots of them before, in the park during the city's recent renovations, and at construction sites in the city. This one was propped up on concrete blocks and had a wood fire burning underneath, tended by two of Hagar's Maenads, some Girl Scouts Senga recognized from the bus.

"Strip," Hagar ordered her, and the girls giggled.

"What?"

"Don't flatter yourself. You heard me. Take off those rags—they need to be burned. And get yourself into that tub; you're lucky it's bath night."

So Senga had her first bath since the bus crash in a dumpster, filled with water that percolated with the grime of who knew how many other women's bodies. But it was warm, and deep enough so that she could submerge herself, and it felt good.

"Use soap," Hagar snapped, passing Senga a sliver of some oily substance that smelled of a familiar something but which Senga couldn't name. "And get your hair too. And hurry up; I haven't got all day." She had already taken Senga's clothes and shoved them into the shallow pit under the dumpster where the fire had almost gone out. It flamed up again, but just enough to keep the water warm—not enough to scorch Senga when her body floated against the sides of the metal tank, hitting them and causing them to emanate a hollow, watery, bonging sound. Hagar was scowling and pointing and saying something to the girls that Senga couldn't hear, and she didn't care to try.

Her body was stirring up warm currents from the fire-heated bottom of the tank, and the warmth was waking her up. The unfamiliarity of what should have been the old sensation of bathing jolted her, and the results of the industriousness of the others began to shake her and make her ashamed. She had thought she would bring welcome news to them. Instead she saw that they hadn't been waiting for her, and that her news was neither welcome, nor was it news. They had begun to live the lives they wanted to live. Senga began to realize that she had been asleep in her bower too long. It was early evening; and as she floated in the tub on her back in the gloaming, she could look up and out between the branches overhead and see the blushing dusk, and a single naked star. Nighttime. It was time to wake up.

CHAPTER THIRTEEN

ABBESS AND ACOLYTES

WHILE SENGA HAD BATHED, THE GIRLS WHO HAD tended the fire were joined by some others, who deftly assisted her out of the tank and into a long, pale garment similar to the ones she had seen the others wearing as she'd approached the Carousel. The coarse fabric, as it passed over her face, gave off a clean scent Senga sharply recognized from childhood, when her mother had hung their household laundry on the roof, to dry in the sun. She sneezed in the light evening breeze, and a sweet-faced, tall-ish girl stepped up with a rough, but similarly immaculate cloth to rub-dry her hair for her, after which a smaller girl began to dress it with some sweet-smelling oil and comb it with a wide-toothed comb. The tall girl gave her clean water to drink. Senga didn't resist, didn't assist. She looked on—as if at something happening to someone else—as she was given a pair of soft fabric shoes for her feet; more like small cloth bags, or socks, really, and then she was led by the smallest of the fire-girls, who took her hand and guided her to where the Abbess sat.

A buzz of activity accelerated as some women readied the Carousel lawn for the gathering, grunting and pulling the heavy wooden benches and long tables into place, but the Abbess, as usual, only ever presided, she did no work. A fire burned in a small clearing on the far side of the Carousel lawn, and a rich smell of roasting meat perfumed the air. Senga realized what it was she had seen Buffy doing to the body of Putty Hair. It was his flesh that had been spitted and was now being turned into a sizzling, reeking meal.

She looked at the Abbess, who smiled and patted the bench nearest her. "We had almost given you up for dead," she said, smiling her dead-eyed smile, and Senga knew suddenly that if she had been caught sleeping in her glade, or if she had fallen into Buffy's trap, it would have been her body they were turning on the spit, without rue or remorse. But she sat down next to the Abbess nonetheless, and smiled, albeit mirthlessly, and although she felt dazed, she determined that she would say nothing. In fact, there was nothing she *could* say. *She* was wandering around like an animal. *They* were building a civilization. What could *she* say to *them*?

The Abbess smoothed out the folds of her linen gown as women began to approach the assembled benches and long tables in front of the Carousel—she would address the gathering before the meal. As Senga looked on, bemused, it seemed to her that time passed quickly, then slowly, then stopped altogether, and the full moon was caught in the branches of the trees that ringed the Carousel lawn. The Abbess patted Senga's hand, and Senga was jolted back into the moment. Again the Abbess's pert nose crinkled. "We'll talk later. I'm sure you have much to ask us, and *we* want to know all about what *you* have been up to, as well." Senga just stared at her, like an owl. The Abbess winked at her, (grotesquely, considering the circumstances, Senga thought) and then rose and crossed to the front of the platform to speak to the gathered crowd in the flesh-scented evening.

Senga remained where she was; she could do little else. She was dazed, and exhausted, and hungry, and she wondered what it was that they were preparing to eat, since an entire person could not, she reasoned, be completely cooked in the time that had elapsed since the killing of Putty Hair. It had taken some time to dress him and spit him and build up the fire; still, from the time she had entered the Carousel clearing she had smelled cooking meat; it was not so long since she had cooked a steak herself that she would have forgotten the smell. Were they preparing something else? But what? What else could they have to prepare? Were there cows? She thought back to that first Full Moon Gathering and her gorge started to rise, but her stomach griped; she might *have* to eat whatever it was, or whoever it was. Putty Hair was one thing, but she would, she thought, draw the line at one of the other women, because . . . well, *you have to draw the line somewhere, don't you?* Nothing was making sense, least of all her own thoughts, but she tried to clear her head, to focus.

She was desperate to know, first of all; had they really started killing and eating *each other*? She squinted hard across the clearing at the spot where Buffy's young helper was turning the spit. Where was Buffy? Senga strained her damaged, monocular vision in the gathering dark and soon she was able to see her, moving hot rocks from the base of the fire to a spot some yards away, adding them to rocks that already smoldered there. So they had a pit-fire as well as the spit; and whatever had been cooking in the pit during the day was probably what they had been preparing to eat that night. Putty Hair was an afterthought, a bonus—a kind of meaty dessert. Senga decided to ignore her stomach until she could see what came out of the pit. She had just about decided that she wouldn't eat anyone she knew. Or anyone younger than ten. (Or thereabouts.) But the pieces of meat the young women were . . .

"Sisters!" the Abbess was saying. "Rejoice! For the great Goddess Mother has answered our prayers, and given us—not just food, but a way forward—we finally have . . . a man—a live one!" Whistles and wolf-calls, *yip, yow-yow-yowwww*, went up from the assembled audience. Of course

126

this announcement was not a surprise; with the return of Buffy and the archers to the Carousel lawn, word had spread like oil across a pane of glass. But the living man was a long-awaited and evidently a long-prayed-for boon. Clearly, the Abbess and her Acolytes had thought long and deeply about the continuation of their world in the woods, and had made real their plans while Senga had *quite literally* (she reproached herself) been sleeping.

Senga turned her head and noticed Buffy and her young helper slapping each other's backs and heard their cries . . . and she also thought she heard notes of anguish in the cries and commotion of the members of the Abbess's audience, cries that went on for some time, to the Abbess's evident pleasure. When the noises began to subside, a medium-sized girl from each of the three long tables padded across the grass to the fire-pit where Buffy and her helper handed each an enormous trencher piled with something grisly and smoking from the rocky oven-pit. Returning laden with the charred meat, the girls stepped up to the dais first and inclined their heads toward the Abbess, who indicated wordlessly that they were to serve the others. She continued to address the crowd as the women ate, pulling meat from bone with scorching fingers, indecorously, like the half-wild hungry things they had become. A girl stepped up onto the dais and handed a bone with some flesh on it, wrapped in a strip of clean cloth, to Senga, who frowned at it. It smelled rank, but her stomach twisted toward it. The Abbess went on.

"It has happened—as it was foretold . . ."

"*You* told us it would," cheered Hagar, and the others repeated after her.

"Told us it would!"

"Tonight we will fill our bellies with the last of our late beloved sister, Mae, who in death has sustained our lives for another day, and for which we give thanks." Heads were bowed throught the assembly. "Tomorrow we will feast on man, for the first time, before our first riding . . . " Senga dropped the hunk of bone as it was halfway to her mouth, and the same small girl who had served it to her scrambled to her feet and grabbed it up. Senga's gorge rose, and her head swam, and she passed out of consciousness for a moment as she leaned against the wall of the Carousel.

The Abbess droned on. The moon had escaped the trees now and bleached the Carousel lawn with its brilliance, staining the grass an icy white and casting blacker-than-black shadows. Buffy continued turning the spit, and wood-against-wood squeaked and squealed.

"We were delivered from the world of men to this world of women in the woods. In a most powerful and awesome way, Our Heavenly Mother delivered us from death and degradation. Through hardship and long toil she has tested us, and now we have proven ourselves worthy. We are ready to receive this boon, and we honor our Mother as we accept her gift. Sleep well tonight sisters, for tomorrow we take the first steps on the road to our destiny."

CHAPTER FOURTEEN

SNATCH

IN THE EVENT, THAT FIRST SNATCH WAS A MESSY AFFAIR, as how could it not have been? It took place, not on the day after the Full of the Moon, as promised, but two days after that. Deeper Voice turned out to have no wish to cooperate in his own demise, and so they'd had to leave him down in the pit for a day or two to wear him out. Even after that, the two women who'd been sent to fetch him out of the trap couldn't quite manage it, and ultimately it was Buffy who grappled with him, finally resorting to getting into the trap herself and half-strangling him, with a beefy knee on his chest, until he lost consciousness. At the edge of the pit, Renee and Alice clutched each other and cried "don't kill him," and "we need him alive!" Finally Buffy hauled him, semi-conscious, out of the pit, using the same rope and pulley she'd used to get the dead Putty Hair out, and lashed him to a sledge that the women had prepared for the task.

Of course, when Deeper Voice regained consciousness, he struggled and thrashed, but the hemp ropes were thick and strongly knotted. Buffy and the two other women took turns dragging the sledge and sitting on Deeper Voice's chest on the road back to the Carousel Lawn, where the rest of the women were picking the remains of Putty Hair out of their teeth.

Senga's plan, insofar as she had one, was to feign contrition and a desire to rejoin the Abbess's group—until she could think of a better one. And so she helped put the finishing touches on the man-cage, the crude device the Abbess had engineered and the women had built out of felled saplings and ropes; if Senga had thought that the forest provided for her needs because it intuited that she was alone and unviolent, she soon had to rethink that notion. The Abbess's followers were embarked on a perverse and deadly quest—even so, the forest had provided them every bit of raw material they needed, as well.

Out of this they had constructed the shelters and huts Senga had seen ringing the Carousel lawn, and they had the metal tanks, the dumpsters, which they used for bathing and cooking. They had the schoolbuses, too, big, late-twentieth-century luxury coaches, out of which they had fashioned both

130

a schoolhouse and a dormitory. In the Carousel itself there was shelter in inclement weather for the entire tribe, and comfort, too. Everyone scavenged, and although there were days when the scavenging parties emerged from the forest and returned to the Carousel Lawn with empty hands, there were evenings enough when they came back with treasures. They needed to dig—they found spades. They needed tools, and the thin edges of the woods gave up a hammer and an axe. A saw was desired, and one was discovered.

The hammer was no good without nails—and lo! They found nails. Cloth for their clothing came from what they surmised had been a warehouse overgrown with vines along the southwestern border of the forest. In fact it had once been a dry goods store situated on a street called Jamaica Avenue, a street that had been swallowed by the forest and before that, riven by the quake, and preserved—seemingly for them to use.

And use it they did. The cataclysm had folded the building in half, like a book. One day it had been discovered by Renee, and the women had raced to plunder it, in their haste collapsing the crooked mezzanine level onto the ground floor. However, no one important was hurt, and they treated the remains the same way they would eventually treat Mae, and Putty Hair, and anyone else who happened to die: as protein.

So Senga was handed some rope and instructed to fortify the cage where Deeper Voice would be kept, naked and bruised, and alive, until he was needed. Her instructions were not to speak to him when she passed him his ration of food. None of the women spoke to him, although his cage was left in the center of the Carousel Lawn for three days. He spoke— he spat, and screamed, and clutched and wrung the bars with filthy hands, and lunged for Senga whenever she brought him his rations. On the second day, the other women began to approach him with sticks, and to poke him through the bars. The smaller girls pelted him with pebbles. But the nubile ones, who were budding and supple—they were scrubbed and softened and sent to entice him, dressed in the diaphanous shifts that were tight over their pink breasts, gliding past his cage with something like mercy in their eyes as they smuggled him berries and eggs. As they had been taught, they caught and gazed into his eyes, and if he had been himself he would have seen what was happening, but it was long since he had been himself. In his despair, he saw a chance to escape in the eager eyes of the blossoming young ones, unaware that what he was seeing was in truth his deeper entrapment. When the bolder of the young girls let her finger stroke his in the gathering dark of the second evening as she deposited her offering of extra food, he believed he had found his accomplice. In truth, she had him. She placed a finger against her lips then reached through the bars and touched his arm, mouthing just one word —"later."

In the deepest part of the night, she came to him with a knife. Her name was Skye. She was naked under a rough blanket, and when she had cut through the rope lashings, she faced her victim and smiled. The moon was past the full, but there was enough light for Senga, where she was hidden, to see what was happening and to play her part. She went to the edge of the lean-to she had been assigned to share and coughed. Loud enough to be heard across the lawn, loud enough to make cover for the young girl to enter the cage to clutch at the arm of the young man who thought she was rescuing him. The girl shook her head, no, and placed a restraining hand on his arm. "Careful," she mouthed, and he nodded. Senga, seemingly awakened from sleep, played out her part. Walking to the edge of the lawn she squatted and pissed.

In the cage, young woman and young man squirmed against each other in the tight quarters, and young flesh called to young flesh. Covering them both with the wooly blanket, the young woman smiled up into Deeper Voice's eyes and reached down between his legs for what she had been told she would find there. Find it she did, and she stroked it to keep it hard as she'd been taught, as she looked directly into his eyes and licked two of her fingers, and held them up to him for him to spit on them, too. He did, and she wiped the resulting mixture against her body's inner walls as she pushed the dazed and weakened young man onto his back and took him into herself. The ride was quick, but he was one of those whose climax could be felt—his thick cock pulsed inside her, once, twice, three times, and he was spent, and she knew he was spent.

Before he caught his breath, his strange partner was out of the cage and away, and Senga and Buffy were lashing the bars shut again. The girl called Skye scampered into the Carousel to cheers and applause, and was given the best bed to sleep in (with the feet propped up to help the spunk she was harboring to do its job).

If Deeper Voice had been a different sort of man, he could have stretched his life out for a few more days, and perhaps even had another rider or two, however, he screamed and cursed so angrily and so much that night that Hagar dispatched him before dawn with a knife between the ribs.

They had to smoke some of his flesh to preserve it, they had such a surfeit.

Over the course of the days that followed, the women celebrated. Of course, Skye was kept in bed; this was an historic first, and care had to be taken. No one wanted a repeat of what had happened back in the beginning, to Senga and Hagar. No one wanted anything to upset the natural order; conception, pregnancy, birth. They would worry about other things later, things like the possibility that the child so conceived could be male. "We'll cross that bridge when we come to it," said The Abbess.

She and her Acolytes were holding court in the best bedchamber of the Carousel with Skye, now, and in groups of twos and threes the rest of the women and girls were ushered in and then ushered out. The bed was piled high with flowers, and some of the girls brought fruits; wild strawberries like the ones Senga had found near her stream; tiny but bright red and bursting-sweet. Grapes were brought, too, from a vine that grew in Guatemala; Hagar had ventured there to offer some of the smoked remains of Deeper Voice to the Guatemalans, which they declined.

Not wishing to cause offense, and desiring nothing more than to be left in peace, the eldest of the Guatemalan women had made an offering, not only of grapes, but of a cutting from the grapevine itself. She was wise; she wanted no more visits from the Abbess's women to blight the lives of her and her friends; she and they wanted to be left alone to live and die unmolested by the attentions of the Abbess and her demented followers, who were like door-to-door saleswomen peddling lipstick. They watched Hagar leave with her companions, and when they were satisfied that she was gone, the Guatemalan women began to strike their camp, and to move deeper into the woods. In times to come they would be seen by the Abbess's followers more and more rarely, and almost forgotten, which suited them.

Senga entered the Carousel to pay respects to Skye in her turn. She wished her well, but it was to the Abbess that she wanted to speak.

"Senga, you performed your part beautifully," the Abbess gushed. Taking their cues from their leader, the Acolytes beamed at this somehow rehabilitated Senga.

"Yeah, well, I didn't know Hagar was gonna kill him."

The Abbess laughed her silvery, tinkling laugh and wrinkled her nose.

"Well, it might have been done more elegantly, but still it would have had to be done."

"Why not just bring him back to the edge of the forest and let him go back to wherever he came from? Why does it have to be killing?" Senga now remembered the first Full Moon Meeting and the meaning of the Rules of the Forest, which she had thought were a joke.

The Abbess chuckled. "What, 'release him into the wild?'" Her retainers laughed.

Senga shrugged.

"Oh Senga, think. How long do you imagine it would be before men were swarming into the forest, to ruin it the way they ruined everything else?" One of the Acolytes snorted.

"Just think how they'd love to have us here, 'poor defenseless women',"

"Ripe for the taking," tsk'd the other, nameless one. Senga looked at the floor.

"Well anyway, thanks for the bath, and the clothes, and everything, but I'm gonna be going now. I'm sure any one of these ladies will be able to take my place next time the moon is full . . . ."

The Abbess excused herself from her coterie with a grim nod, and walked toward the curtained wall of the bedchamber with Senga.

136

"Consider," she said meaningfully, placing a restraining hand on Senga's arm.

"I have done nothing but," said Senga, removing it.

If the buses had not crashed, and the world had not ended, if the Abbess had taken her place in the society that was now finished, she might have said something to Senga like, "I'm offering you an opportunity to get in on the ground floor of something big." For truly, those were the terms in which the Abbess thought. The forest was to her a golden opportunity to impose her will on everyone in it. Senga smiled a crooked, close-lipped smile. "No thanks," she said, as if reading the Abbess's thoughts. "I'll be going *now.*" She slipped out of the Carousel and made her way slowly back toward her glade by the stream and the rockfall. She would begin again there.

CHAPTER FIFTEEN

RELAY STATION DAYS

ANOTHER WOMAN DID TAKE SENGA'S PLACE, AND Buffy dug more holes to trap more men. At the next full of the moon there were two wooden cages in the clearing on the Carousel Lawn, with two new men howling and shaking the bars. Three girls had begun to bleed in addition to Skye, whose pregnancy seemed to be established, and so the three would take turns riding the captives, and Hagar was under strict orders that no matter how loudly they protested, she was to leave at least one man alive until each girl had ridden at least once. It was left to Senga to wonder how much the Abbess had foreseen and how much she had engineered, during those first few months when she had first had the idea of the Snatch. Back when Senga had stumbled onto the first Full Moon Meeting—that's at least how far back this plan went. As she walked back to her redoubt, Senga realized that she had let contempt for the Abbess blind her to the woman's intelligence. She would be doubly on her guard now, and in future, she promised herself.

The Guatemalans were rewarded by the forest for their move to a safer site; they had fresh water and fertile soil, and if the vegetarian diet on which they mainly subsisted sometimes seemed flat, they could always eke it out with eggs and small game. Never would they resort to eating anything from the other women, *las mujeres malas,* even when it was offered to them by the playful, wild-haired little girl who sometimes appeared at their camp, pointing at herself and saying "Yuki-Kai." She came and went like an animal, a feral thing, and the Guatemalan women made a pet of her, but they never trusted that the food she carried in a small sack slung over her shoulder hadn't recently been human.

Senga went back to her bower, where she constructed a shelter like the ones she had observed at the Carousel Lawn. She talked to herself, said the women the Abbess sent to check on her periodically, and the Abbess smiled sadly and shook her head as if to say "poor thing," but she kept sending the women to check.

It was to this bower that Maureen would come when she was in labor with Pink, and it was to the Guatemalans that Maureen went to die, and they buried her in their little churchyard. Neither Senga nor Pink ever knew where she went. Anything could happen in that forest; anything did. Animals and birds died and became food for other animals, Maureen was just a big, two-legged animal, after all. The forest must have eaten her up.

So Pink and Yuki grew up in the forest, motherless girls, side-by-side, but ignorant of each other, the one kept in secret by Senga, the other subjected to the Abbess's rule. Pink had never been hit. Yuki-Kai was beaten frequently, and with great ceremony, for all kinds of infractions, until Hagar's arm was sore, but the beatings only seemed to drive the wildness further into the core of her being instead of casting it out.

Pink and Senga moved into the Relay Station when Pink was an infant, and Senga felt relief; here they would be safer. At least they would be drier, for when summer came to the forest, it brought monsoonal rains the likes of which Senga had never experienced before. The red tile roof kept them dry, and in the old, white-tiled kitchen, there was a large stove, which of course was no longer gasified, but which was still fireproof. Senga taught Pink how to make "cats" out of paper and twigs, and allowed her to help light the fires that warmed them and made the wet winters bearable.

They celebrated Christmas in the relay station every year—Senga would chop the uppermost section from a small conifer and bring it indoors, upon the branches of which, at first, she alone, then she and Pink together, would hang things they had found, to each other's delight. Pink favored the shiny wrappers from chewing gum that she would find when Senga took her walking. Senga loved bird's nests. And on Christmas Eve, Senga would rock her girl to sleep, singing "Silent Night," until Pink's dreams could almost be seen, setting her paper-thin eyelids fluttering. "Merry Christmas," Senga would whisper in the echoing dark, before daring to fall asleep herself, one arm around her foster-daughter, and one ear open. That's how it went, for a long time. Winters brought to Senga and Pink their thin imitations of Christmases past.

When snow fell in the forest, the black trunks of the trees and their blacker branches stood out starkly against the mysteriously violet sky. Then Senga kept Pink indoors, in the Relay Station, not only for warmth, but because the naked trees gave no cover; it would have been possible to see long distances, and Senga distrusted the Abbess.

Indoors, of course, there was no television as Senga had enjoyed as a child in winter, when her father, a bricklayer, would be released early from work. Mortar wouldn't adhere to the bricks when the wet snow fell, and so home he would come, stamping his feet in his workboots with their complicated hooks and leather laces, shedding his cold, wet clothes until he was down to the socks his mother-in-law had knitted him, and something called "combination underwear." He'd sip whisky and watch television with Senga, his spicy male smell warm and comforting as he'd let her burrow into the crook of his arm, and her mother would cover them both with a blanket she'd made herself, of a kaleidoscopic array of

141

odd bits of yarn left over from sweaters and other projects. Outside, the violet light made the sky magical, and inside the blue-grey light from the television flickered and jumped in time with the lights that bubbled on the family's Christmas tree. Senga missed her father. Her mother, too, she supposed.

Here in the now, she couldn't watch television at Christmas in a cozy apartment under a blanket with Pink, but there were books in the forest, and Pink learned to read them at Senga's knee. Sometimes Senga read them to her in the fading winter light.

Some of the books Senga had found in her explorations of the Relay Station while the infant Pink was asleep; most of these had been left behind in the bathrooms, along with what used to be called "girlie" magazines. Senga burned these in the stove; she didn't want Pink to see them. She didn't want to see them herself; not because she disapproved—quite the contrary. But what good would it do her to get, as she put it, "turned on," when there was little chance of being turned off again in the way she preferred, in a feather bed, by a hairy-legged man, not too tall, heavily muscled, with dark eyes and a smile that could make the angels weep. She laughed at herself as she burned the magazines and said, "Sayonara, sex."

Senga devised games as Pink grew, games to train her to survive, like "the pain game," and games to occupy her curious, growing mind. Like all children, Pink asked "why" about things Senga could explain and about things she

142

couldn't—and about things Senga wouldn't explain. Pink learned to be satisfied with whatever Senga told her. She had to.

A game they both loved to play was one they called "Alphabet." In this game, Pink sat between Senga's legs with her back to Senga, who traced letters with her index finger on Pink's small, straight back. Pink learned quickly, and soon progressed to spelling out entire words, then sentences, as Senga wrote them on her skin. In fact, she soon surpassed Senga's ability to "read" the words spelled out on her own back by Pink. This delighted both of them.

She taught Pink to read and write, with materials provided by the forest, or rather by those who had left them behind for the forest to unearth. Right after the initial cataclysm, when the forest had begun eating up larger and larger patches of Brooklyn and Queens, the roots of the fast-growing trees churned up everything in their path, breaking through asphalt and tilling whatever they found underneath. The trees chewed through all, including sewers and gas lines and garbage dumps; and it was from these last that many of the raw materials that Senga and the other women lived on came.

There had been a small public library building near the old store that was the source of much of what the women plundered, and the books it contained might have been easy enough for Senga to bring back to the Relay Station, except for two problems. One was that the pool of books was never wide enough, so Senga was forced to be careful in selecting classics for both herself and Pink; the second problem was, as she discovered, that paper, like water, was heavier than it looked, and difficult to carry. And then of course the forest itself seemed determined to consume the library building, and pitted itself against Senga, pulling down more and more of the building day by day, blocking the windows with creeping ivy and liana-like vines faster than Senga could rip them out, until finally she had to admit defeat—the books she had managed to salvage would have to do. And they did.

CHAPTER SIXTEEN

BROOKLYN

MOST OF THOSE WHO HAD LIVED IN BROOKLYN had died quickly once the estuarial waters of the East River rose up and commingled with the lagoon that had been Jamaica Bay. The higher reaches of Staten Island were spared, but tiny Governor's Island was devoured entirely by the flood as it washed eastward, engulfing Red Hook, Park Slope and all of Carroll Gardens. Borough Park went under, and most of Brooklyn south and west of Bensonhurst—including Coney Island, Sheepshead Bay, and Brighton Beach—was gone, as well. What was left of Brooklyn now began somewhere in the vicinity of what had been Crown Heights and stretched south to Midwood, which now sat on the oily shore of what had been Gravesend Bay. Bedford Stuyvesant was spared the flooding, as were Cypress Hills and East New York, but the fires, which raged for several years after the cataclysm, destroyed much that had escaped the flood. The northeastern fringe of Prospect Park, where it was joined to the forest, became the boundary between the remains of Brooklyn and the once teeming, now eerily vacant no-man's-land of Fort Greene, Clinton Hill, Williamsburg and Greenpoint. Everything else was forest and flood.

Brooklyn had been filled with fuel—banks and offices filled with paper, and courthouses, warehouses, markets, museums, and buildings that burned, and burned, and burned. Structures collapsed, as the earth had convulsed, and there was no green forest able to gain purchase in the rocks and cobbles that remained of the streets. What had been Brooklyn became a moonscape, inhabited by distrustful, warring tribes scrabbling for survival and supremacy. It was from among these that the Women of the Woods hunted Spunk, as the Abbess had foreseen and foretold.

These survivors, too—men *and* women—scavenged along the old roads, but the forest was anathema to them. It was, they said, "haunted." But their young ones, daring each other, would brave the forest's thin eaves, which was perfect for the purposes of the Women of the Woods. That's what Deeper Voice and Putty Hair had been up to that proved to be their undoing. That's what the young men from what had been Brooklyn *kept* doing, and that's what kept the Women in the Woods hunting them.

It was almost too easy.

Old Parry was fit, but nowhere near the man he had been, especially when he was in his cups. His son, Young Parry, took after him in build; they were both short (Old Parry was shorter), and the word that came to mind upon first seeing either of them was "hard." Stocky, muscular, working-men's bodies were what they both had; father and son had the same broad shoulders tapering in a V to their waists, flat bellies, and heavily muscled glutes, and thighs that led down to wiry calves. When they stood, side-by-side the way they did, with their arms folded across their chests, and hands tucked into their armpits, from the back they were hard to tell apart. The young Parry was slighter, as young people are, and the old Parry's hair was white, but they had come, as people said, from the same mold. Young Parry's mother, Old Parry's wife, was dead, and all the two men had were each other.

"Haunted, my arse," Old Parry was slurring, "that forest is filled with real, live human beings, and they have been preying on our young'uns for too long. We should torch it."

Some of his listeners nodded agreement, but there were more who demurred.

"You have no proof," said a man older than Old Parry, who had been a church sexton or vicar, and was therefore considered the spiritual leader of their group. Considered by himself, at least. Anyway, he spoke of peace and order, and the others usually listened to him.

"And you have no sons!" Old Parry thundered, clapping his son's shoulder with one of his hard, pink, hands. "It's only ever our sons that get taken!"

"You mean it's only ever our sons who are foolish enough to venture into the woods," said a woman who had lost a son to the forest herself last year. "We tell them and tell them, but they won't take a telling! My Jamey was a good boy, but he wouldn't listen, God rest his soul."

"Who knows what's in there," said someone else. "There could be animals, or anything. It doesn't mean there's people there, alive or dead! Forests are dangerous places, anyway—always have been!"

"Aye, this one is," grunted Parry, finishing his drink and banging the glass on the table. One word borrowed another, and the group's discussion quickly degenerated into insults and shouting.

"You mark me," said Old Parry, rising to leave, "the time is coming when I'll do something about it myself, if you won't. They won't get my son!" He swayed, and his son was there to steady him.

"Come on, Pop. Time to go." Young Parry knew better than to suggest that his father had had too much to drink; it was better to let him come to that conclusion himself. Young Parry dug in his trousers pockets and flipped a coin he found

148

there towards the sexton, who also ran this little tavern that was one of the Brooklynites gathering places.

"Don't you think of it," Old Parry gripped his son's hand as the younger man put him to bed. They had been living lately in the ruins of the Broadway Junction elevated train station, a broken steel and concrete labyrinth in the air, on the northeastern tip of the remaining inhabitable sliver of East New York. But no one in Brooklyn lived anywhere for very long. They were nomads, and scavengers, too, maintaining a rough urbanity even in the extremity of their situation. This was a favorite spot of theirs despite its proximity to the forest, but Old Parry had almost made up his mind not to return to it any more, now that his son was of Disappearing Age.

"I won't think of it, Pop." Young Parry crooned as he smoothed his father's white, white, downy hair over his hard, round head. Old Parry closed his eyes. But think of it Young Parry did.

He hadn't stopped thinking about it since the last time he'd ventured into the forest and come out again. No one had seen him, he thought.

But he had seen someone. He had seen *her*. He had seen Pink.

It had been several weeks ago, before the argument in the tavern. He had been walking along the old tracks of the elevated train that had bisected the borough, tracks that almost disappeared, then boldly reappeared, and ended in a stairway with steps that led downward.

A green, ferny profusion of leaves and the composty earth in which they grew had almost obliterated the old steps, turning them into a slippery ramp, and because he was so excited he wasn't paying attention, Young Parry slid all the way down to the foot of it, coming to a painful stop against a wall of vegetation. The woods. As he recovered his footing and attempted to climb back up to the train tracks in the air, he noticed a movement down by his feet. An invisible hand was parting the thorny shrubs for him, and without planning to, he put first his head, then his shoulders, into the widening gap, and as soon as he could get his legs into the opening, he found he could stand in a widening clearing. He looked over his shoulder; he could see the steps that led up to the train tracks and safety. He turned and looked ahead; the opening was getting wider, parting like grass before a cyclone, inviting him in.

A house of pale yellow brick with a red tile roof peeked through the trees beyond the tangled mass of swiftly parting brambles. A shaft of yellowest sunlight pierced the clouds above and the forest canopy below and drew his eye to an upper window of that house, and in that upper window was a girl, golden and rosy. She was beautiful, with a beauty worth dying to see and hold, and Young Parry was lost. He moved forward toward her, but she was called away from the window, and the sunlight faded, and the brambles began to sigh and crack around his legs. He turned his head—he could still see the steps that led back to safety, and he ran for them, falling against them as the briar hedge snapped shut behind him.

CHAPTER SEVENTEEN

HOW PINK WAS HURT

RUNNING THE LAST FEW HUNDRED FEET, SENGA PELTED into the Relay Station, frantic. Her eyes were wide as she made her way back to the rooms Pink had picked for herself. Pink's screams had subsided to moans, now, and she held herself around her middle and gave voice to her pain and betrayal as Senga took her into her arms and rocked her to and fro on the floor until the spasm of grief subsided. She took Pink's face into both of her hands and wiped back the blazing strands of hair that so mesmerised Yuki-Kai.

"What happened, my love?"

Pink couldn't say. She had tricked Senga, and she had paid a price. Her breath shuddered out of her. Now she too knew shame. She had lost her innocence—not by means of her sex game with Yuki—that was almost incidental. Her innocence, which Senga had trusted in, had gone the moment Pink had started to keep the secret of Yuk-Kai; the thing of her own that Senga knew nothing about.

"Someone else did this to you," Senga said to her, evenly, when her tears had subsided. Pink nodded, sniffling. "What I need to know *right now* is not who, or why, but if we are in danger from that someone."

Pink shook her head violently, no, her massy, red ringlets flying, her breath shuddering into and out of her as she labored to calm herself.

"Okay," said Senga, her mind racing, but her demeanor cool. "Lie down and let me see you. You don't have to tell me anything. Just let me see how you're hurt." But as Pink lay down and allowed Senga's hands to begin examining her, she did tell her, everything. When the girl was finished talking, Senga smiled her crooked, rueful smile and said, "I might have known. That Yuki-Kai is a menace." Senga shook her head. "Huh. There's hope for her yet."

By this time she had stripped off Pink's undergarments and washed between her legs with clean water; she'd had no time to heat it, so Pink shivered as the cold liquid touched her delicate flesh. "Looks like she got you with one of her nails," Senga said, lifting and looking at one of the pink leaflike folds that bled profusely even though the wound was not deep. "the thumb, I guess. Keep that clean," she instructed, "Yuki's nails are probably filthy."

"Thank you, Senga," said Pink, suddenly shy of this woman, who had fed her and raised her and kept her from harm, and who even now could surprise her.

"I mean it. The worst thing would be to get an infection; we wouldn't be able to do anything about that, and it's a nasty way to die." Senga bustled as she spoke, putting away the water bowl and the washcloth, and Pink surprised her when she suddenly, wordlessly grabbed her and knocked her breathless as she encircled her waist from behind. She was nearly as tall as Senga now, and she wriggled around to face her without removing her arms from Senga's waist.

"Well," said Senga, when she'd recovered her breath, "as my mother once said to me, and as her mother once said to her, 'now you know the big secret.'" At the word "mother" she balked, a momentary slip. That was not a word she and Pink used often.

Pink nodded her head, which was buried in the crook of Senga's neck. Senga lifted the young girl's chin and looked into her eyes. "Yuki might mean well, or she might be so mad at you that she wants to hurt you even more—we can't know. But what I do know for certain is that two people can keep a secret—if one of them is dead."

"No, Senga!"

154

"I don't mean we need to do anything to Yuki, don't worry about that. But I'm telling you— this is trouble. Do you love her?"

Pink shrugged and shook her head and mumbled something that sounded like "I dunno. Not really."

Senga sighed. It was long past time for her to do what she had to do now. She would tell Pink everything, and Pink would understand. They would get ready to leave quickly; they'd walk through the forest and find a way out. Senga had wanted to use one of her tunnels—the way she had figured it, until she was sure of what she might find in the World Outside, she wanted to be able to get back into the forest if they needed to. She and Pink might not be able to live out there. Walking out of the forest was riskier, and at the end they'd have to hack their way through. They couldn't count on getting out unnoticed, either. The tunnels would have offered the advantage of secrecy. Except . . . . Senga shook her head. She didn't want to think about it.

So instead, she took Pink by the hand and led her out into their garden, and told her their story, the story of them, from the very beginning. The buses, the crash, the drivers, the women, the Snatch, Maureen—everything. Pink's eyes widened, and narrowed, and her brows knitted together, and it was well after dusk when Senga had finally finished telling her tale. In the gathering darkness she peered at her foster daughter hopefully, but couldn't read the expression on her face. But Pink's hand had gone still in Senga's hand, and that wasn't a good sign.

"I'm sorry, Pink," she lifted one shoulder. "I couldn't let them have you. But I didn't think this far ahead . . . ."

"You lied to me!" shouted the young liar, with all the indignation of her youth. "And you had no right to keep me from my real mother!" The mercury in Pink's thermometer exploded. "I hate you!" she cried, as capriciously and forcefully as she had embraced Senga in filial love, earlier. "I'm going to find Yuki-Kai. And I never want to see you again."

"Pink, no . . ."

But it was too late. Over the garden wall of dry-stacked stone Pink leapt, and Senga was too old, and too exhausted and too brokenhearted to catch her. She couldn't call out to her, and she couldn't ask the others for help. She wandered in the dark as far as she dared, then came back to the Relay Station, collapsed, and slept where she lay that evening. Morning would come soon enough, and bring with it its own problems. *Protect her,* Senga pleaded silently. *Heavenly Mother, protect her.*

CHAPTER EIGHTEEN
MIDWIFERY

I N THE INTERVENING YEARS BETWEEN THE FIRST SNATCH and Pink's long-delayed explosion, there had been stretches of time when every infant born in the forest was female, and then the tenderest meat was missing from the stew pots. During some years, the meat the Abbess and her followers lived on was stringy and tough, and came from older men who had followed young ones into the forest for their own purposes, and found themselves in one of Buffy's traps. Of course, every man who found his way into the forest—young or old—came to an end in the stew pot or on the spit; some simply got there sooner rather than later.

The traps were of three kinds; there were pits of two sorts, and snares, and there were several rings of them around the part of the forest controlled by the Abbess. One type of pit was staked; at first it had been thought necessary to guard the forest against any intruders—however as it became clear that the forest had ways of defending itself, construction of this type of trap was abandoned. Buffy had been instructed to fill them in on her rounds, but sometimes she forgot.

This left a relatively unprotected portion of the forest around the Relay Station—seen from above, a map of the trap system would have looked like a map of the long-destroyed state of Michigan, with Pink and Senga residing in what would have been the webbing between thumb and fingers.

Senga used snare traps as well, to catch small game, like chipmunks and squirrels, but the snares Buffy constructed to the Abbess's design were huge, the better to catch men. It was easier to subdue men caught in this way, for some unknown reason, and less likely to damage the men's reproductive organs, which was an important consideration. The pit traps were easier to maintain, of course, not having to be re-set after each successful use, but sometimes Buffy missed one on her rounds, and the men caught in it died, and by the time she found them, they had putrefied, and were no good for either spunk or meat. When that happened, Buffy would surreptitiously fill the hole, transforming it into a grave, and dig another nearby—although Buffy could have killed the Abbess with one blow from the back of her sizeable right hand, she was afraid of her and of her authority. Her authority, her temper and her rages, which flared up more and more frequently as the years went on. Several gaps opened up in the ring of traps in this manner, as the ones Buffy missed tended to be located near each other, and the new pits she dug had to be considerably further away from the sides of the old pit, or they would collapse.

Whenever the proportion of boy babies to girl babies born was commensurate with what it had been in the World Before, that was still a good year for the Abbess—in the world before the crash, more boys had always been born than girls, but fewer boys survived. In the World of the Woods, none did.

At first, and at Buffy's suggestion, the women had tried a sort of rough-and-ready castration technique that involved twine and a sharp knife, but the results were predictable: death by exsanguination (and a complete refusal of the butchers to ever attempt anything like it again). Hagar had opposed this experiment anyway, on the grounds that Buffy was an idiot, and that "a boy without a penis is just a boy without a penis—cutting it off doesn't make him a girl, any more than blindfolding someone's eyes makes them blind." Much easier on the killers' consciences were the slow starvation of the boy babies (left deep in the forest where their ever-weaker cries wouldn't bring down the useless milk in their mothers' breasts), the painful, punitive binding of those young mothers' breasts, and the ceremonial feasts that followed.

The women had divided themselves according to the tasks they performed. The butchers, of course, taught by Buffy, dressed the men and spitted them. The farmers-and-gatherers, Maenads led by Hagar, grew crops and also scavenged. Early on they had found wild onions and lemongrass, and the strawberries that grew along the old roadway. From what had been the very edge of the forest's border with Brooklyn, they stumbled into the remains of a householder's garden, containing numerous tomato vines and some wild runner beans, potatoes, and eggplants, too, along with what Hagar called a "Mary on the Half-Shell," a plaster statue of a woman, standing on a globe of the earth, crushing the head of a snake with her sandaled foot. Her head was covered with a white mantle, and her gown was blue and long, and modestly draped. She held her hands out with the palms upturned, in a gesture halfway between welcome and supplication. "A what?" asked a small girl on the day they found her.

"Never mind," Hagar snapped, momentarily disconcerted. Even when she had counted herself a Christian, she had never been a "Mary-worshipper," and, now, as one of these particular women in this particular forest, she wasn't sure how she was supposed to feel about what the figure represented, a woman whose usage as a vessel had always seemed to Hagar to place her in the first rank of the world's great female doormats. It was difficult to think of her when praying to the Goddess. Perhaps that is why Hagar prayed to the Goddess less and less.

"Leave it alone," she snarled at the girls, who were beginning to pull and paw at it, loosening it from its bathtub-grotto. "Take all the vegetables you can carry and bring them back to the cooks; bring some to the farmers so they can use the seeds. The Abbess will let you know what we want to do with the statue."

The Abbess knew exactly what she wanted done with the Mary in the forest. "Bury it."

"It's half-buried already," said Hagar. The Abbess's voice was icy-crisp, the individual words she spoke sinking into Hagar's head with condescending clarity:

"Then it should be twice as easy to bury completely."

When the Abbess was in this mood, there were only one or two ways to deal with her. Distractedly, Hagar rubbed her jaw. "Will do," she said, and left, before the second of the two methods was called for.

There had been a licensed practical nurse on one bus, and so she had become the *de facto* medicine woman. Of course, the women all had access to Buffy's pharmacopeia, and there were willow trees in the forest whose bark the nurse combined with small amounts of wild meadowsweet to relieve fevers and simple aches and pains.

It was this practical nurse, whose name was Jessie, who pointed out early on that the sanitary supplies the women had brought with them were quite inadequate, and out of spare clothing and scraps she invented a kind of padded, cloth envelope that buttoned onto the women's and girl's undergarments and served as a serviceable hygienic pad (the first several were filled with batting from the bus seats). Using Jessie's prototype as a template, each woman who needed one sewed her own (except for the Abbess, of course) and in time, although Jessie's invention was washable and re-usable, they began filling their "envelopes" with the scraps of soft paper and fabric that Senga brought them during her trips back to their civilization. She traded paper and rags for vegetables, thus eking out her own and Pink's diet and providing it with some variety.

Before and after Pink came to her, Senga spent some portion of every week (she still counted weeks, as did the other women; it was easy to do and kept them somewhat happily organized) traveling to the northeastern edge of the forest and digging the large tunnel she hoped to use to escape back to the world someday. Even if the world of her memory had been destroyed, the thought that it might not have been, and the effort of trying to reach it both soothed and strengthened her, until the tunnels became too dark, and too deep. She had dug many testing tunnels around the rim of the forest near the Relay Station and it was in the northeast corner that the forest seemed most willing to let her in. That suited her, as it positioned the Relay Station between the tunnel entrance and the Carousel.

162

To protect against cave-ins and keep the way open, Senga shored up the tunnel with bits of wood that she scavenged, and in places, bits of tile that came off the interior walls of the Relay Station—there had been men's and women's shower rooms, and locker rooms, and toilets, and these Senga quarried for tile. Some rooms in the relay station were gutted down to the outer shell, until the station itself, in parts, was in danger of collapse. And if she had only known it, Senga had almost tunneled all the way out of the forest when the last cave-in had nearly killed Pink and herself, and scared her into abandoning the idea of a tunnel escape.

Every woman ate, so every woman farmed (except the Abbess), and each one had a small garden patch near her own shelter. The tomatoes and runner beans were transplanted successfully, and grew easily and well. The potatoes flourished but the eggplants were thick-skinned and unappetizing. Of course there were mushrooms, as in all forests, but being fungus they had little nutritive value. Small game was never abandoned, but used more and more as a garnish, or a seasoning; the men and boys caught for the Snatch provided ample protein. Only the Abbess was ever seen cracking open the bones and sucking the marrow; it was really the only unsightly thing she ever did, and she did it in private, in the Carousel. "My guilty pleasure," she smiled at her reflection in the broken, fly-specked, gilt-framed mirror that sheathed the remains of the Carousel's ancient calliope. Her reflection smiled back at her.

It was almost nine months after that first Snatch, in which the girl named Skye had conceived, that the midwives debuted in their roles. Surprisingly, it was not Jessie, but Hagar who took the lead. With a Maenad as an apprentice, she had prepared what she would need from plans in her head, made up of everything she knew of or remembered about labor and delivery—her father had been a doctor and a collector of medical books, and she had spent many transfixed hours poring over his collection, which, fortunately tended toward the antique and obscure. She used the knowledge so gained during the months of Skye's pregnancy to prepare what tools she could; chiefly a birthing chair and an obstetrical fillet.

On one of Senga's first trading trips, when she brought paper and rags to the Carousel Lawn to trade for vegetables, Hagar had been out in front of her shelter, fashioning the chair from a suitable log. Senga, a basket of vegetables balanced on one hip, stopped to watch her.

"Where'd you get the mallet?"

Hagar paused only briefly to indicate, with a stretch of her neck and a head-toss, somewhere out there, in the thin edge of the woods. She wiped sweat from her forehead awkwardly, with her upper arm.

"The old store. It must have sold everything. I got a packet of sewing needles there once."

Senga grunted agreement. "Yeah. I got beeswax. What are you making?"

Hagar told her.

"So that girl's still . . .".

"Pregnant."

Like Senga, Hagar had miscarried the child she'd conceived with the driver. It was a rueful bond, and one to which they rarely alluded.

"You'd better go back and see if the store sold sandpaper. That wood looks rough."

Hagar snorted, and allowed herself a half-smile. Why, she wondered, was Senga such a pain? They might have been friends.

As if she were thinking the same about Hagar, Senga shifted the basket from her hip to her shoulder uncomfortably.

"See ya," she said.

"See ya," said Hagar.

In the event, Hagar turned out to have a knack for midwifery; the girl Skye was almost at term when her water broke, and Hagar's birthing chair was finished just in time to be put to use. The girl's undeveloped hips were slim, but Hagar plied the fillet with skill, and afterwards, there was a new baby girl in the forest.

"I'll call her—"

"Nova," said the Abbess, sweeping into the shelter where a moment before, Hagar's apprentice had placed the newborn into its mother's arms. She pounced on the infant and held her aloft, as proudly as if she had borne her herself. Her smile was almost too broad. Her browless eyes bulged unpleasantly in the moonlight.

"No-vah," repeated the ubiquitous Acolytes gathered outside. It was a tight fit in the birthing shelter, especially when the Abbess turned to face Hagar, her nightgown swirling around her. "Well done," she said, beaming. Skye lay back, spent and sore, with an expression of stupefied confusion. How quickly had her star become tinsel; for nine months she had been worshipped, and now, it seemed, she was to be ignored.

The Abbess flounced out of the confines of the shelter with the newborn in her arms, and the Acolytes followed her to the center of the clearing. Although it was deep nighttime, news that Skye was in labor had spread to every woman and girl around the Carousel Lawn, and they were clustered outside, waiting for the Abbess to bring them what they had waited for. And in the sudden stark desolation of the birthing shelter, Skye heard the name she would never have picked for her daughter shouted aloud. Hagar sighed, and began to perform her ablutions between the girl's legs as Skye looked down at her silently, in grave puzzlement. Hagar felt something like sympathy for the child, but still had work to do.

"Put your hands on your belly, like I showed you, and push down."

"It feels gross. It's all . . . wobbly. . ." Skye protested. Hagar grabbed the apprentice by the arm and dragged her to

166

the bed. She placed one of the apprentice's hands roughly onto Skye's collapsing belly.

"Find the uterus, and push it down to where it's supposed to be," she instructed through clenched teeth. "And massage it so she doesn't bleed too much." The apprentice, grimacing, did as she was told, and Hagar put the kettle on for tea.

So Skye spent her first hours as a mother listening to the women outside worshipping her child while Hagar took pains to see that she would be fit to ride again soon. She'd proven she was fertile. That was the main thing.

Almost every month after that first Snatch, if there were girls who had begun to bleed, and fresh men in the traps in the woods, there would be a riding. Because women and girls who live in community will begin to bleed at the same time each month, the ridings, or Snatches, became a regular event around which the society of the forest began to be organized.

And so the women were kept busy. Traps had to be checked, cages built and rebuilt, clothes made and mended, goods scavenged or bartered for from Senga, Maenads instructed, men slaughtered, vegetables grown, and harvested, and cooked. What they couldn't get from Senga, the women got for themselves, from the almost-but-somehow-never-quite-exhausted store at the edge of the forest. There were fires going day and night, and these had to be watched by the most trusted of the women. No one who was a fire-watcher was permitted near Buffy's pot plantation or her still; although the women had no moral qualms about intoxication, they had a sense of self-preservation and they knew that the stoners, though well-meaning, couldn't be trusted.

When the infants began to be born in numbers, there was more work to do; the sorting of boy from girl baby was handled as quickly and cleanly as could be arranged; Buffy and the stoners attended to the males, bringing them squirming and squalling to the dying field and then carrying their tiny corpses, stiff and still, back to the stew pots. One year the number of men caught and ridden was low, and Buffy suggested letting the boy babies grow a bit bigger in order to provide more meat, but this idea was shouted down by even the other stoners. "We're not running a fucking nursery school/abbatoir" was the general sentiment. Buffy was wounded by this; all her ideas were shot down.

As the first child, Nova, began to toddle, she was joined by Starla, Diamante, and Melisande; if their mothers had had any ideas about naming them, the Abbess had disabused them of these notions with dispatch, as she had done to Skye.

Over the next years, a fad for flower names came into fashion. These years brought the twins, Rosie and Posie (not strictly a flower, but a name for a bunch of them), a tiny, squalling thing the Abbess named Violet, and plain snub-nosed Daisy. Bible names came into fashion briefly and then disappeared, but not before Tabitha and Sarah were named.

Then came names remembered from the Abbess's female friends and relations from the World Before, names like Barbara, and, Meryl, and Bea, and Maureen, the last of whom would one day grow up to become the mother of Pink.

Chapter Nineteen

Pink Unbound

Pink had lived a bounded and tramelled life, and although only that morning she had argued for more freedom, nonetheless she found herself astonished by the bigness and darkness of the forest outside the Relay Station, once she was outside in it. It was so much *more*—bigger, noisier, darker, and almost-altogether alien than it had seemed from her window, or than it was under the sun. She was almost overcome by the sensation that she was drowning at the bottom of a vast ocean of darkness; she knew she couldn't outrun the feeling, yet she began to try.

The fallen leaves and dry twigs underfoot crackled disquietingly and she began to wish she had paid more attention on her trips to and from the tunnel mouth with Senga. Where *was* she? Above all, she wished she had put on a pair of shoes. Then she wished she had brought some food with her. The ground was stony, her feet were sore, her stomach was growling, it was getting cold, and the dark was entirely unfamiliar. She blamed Senga. "It's the way she raised me. She stole me from my mother and she kept me like a prisoner in that stupid place . . . ." . She looked behind her and was dismayed when she couldn't make out the shape of that stupid place in the forbidding dark.

She widened her eyes, unconsciously, and then consciously narrowed them—still she couldn't discern her surroundings—surely Senga would come to look for her. But Senga was sleeping where she had fallen, worn out with age and worry and the strain of the previous day. When Senga didn't wake up and look for her daughter, anger, outrage, misery, and panic all chased each other across Pink's mind and left their traces quivering in her body.

In the Relay Station, she and Senga had had candles to light their nights—Pink was entirely unprepared for the grim and unalleviated blackness of the forest night. After whining and dithering for some time, she collapsed—as dramatically as she could, in case Senga *were* following her after all—and began to whimper, but her heart wasn't in it. In spite of her fear and discomfort, deep inside she was alive with the buds of exhilaration, of approaching destiny, of *becoming* that is the very essence and character of youth. When it became clear that Senga was not coming after her, she decided. She would let Senga worry about her for one night, before she'd go back. That would show *her*.

As in her mind's eye Pink planned her victorious return to the no-doubt stricken and suitably chastened Senga, she lullabyed herself with images of her triumphant homecoming. She fell asleep, not very far from the stream and the strawberry patch where the first men had broken into the forest, almost on the same spot where Senga, before her, had slept when she, too, could go no more.

Yuki-Kai, too, was escaping. After the incident in the classroom and Glynis's awkward tears, she'd decided to return to Pink, to apologize. It would be easy to go on from there to Guatemala, and if Pink wouldn't go with her, she would go on her own. She had been there many times before. She wasn't going back to the others, she was certain of that. She was her own woman now.

She was on her way now, and better prepared than Pink was, to be out in the forest in the dark, stealthily melting into the nightshade that grew around the buses. She had stopped to put on shoes, and she had sleeve of crackers she had planned to gorge on privately when she'd lifted them earlier that day from the common store; they were still wrapped in crinkly paper, just as they had come from the shelf in the old department store on Jamaica Avenue, and they were dry and hard, having survived unopened for all the years since the breaking of the world. But she had eaten crackers from that store before; she liked the salty, flaky, crumbling dryness between her teeth, and at least they were free of mold. The ones she had eaten before had done her no harm. Anyway, once she arrived at the Relay Station, she would get some food from Pink and Senga's stores, and in Guatemala food had never been a problem. The stolen crackers were just to add to her sense of adventure and panache.

Having wrapped herself in a blanket as she slipped away from the buses where the Maenads slept, Yuki-Kai felt bold and free as she crept through the familiar night, past the outlying shelter where Buffy snored and hiccupped, sleeping her noisy, drunken, innocent sleep.

Across the shallow, wooded valley, in the Carousel, Hagar and the Abbess turned their backs to one another in bed as they struggled to find their separate ways into the maze of oblivion. They had argued; it had become physical. The Abbess's rule, which Hagar had always observed, was "not in the face." Hagar understood—she even agreed; after all, it would be difficult to command the necessary respect from the rest of the women in the woods while sporting a burst eyelid, or a bruised lip, or even a nail-scratched cheek. And of course, some of the obeisance the others showered on the Abbess had always splashed onto Hagar too, as her lieutenant. But the Abbess needed to watch her step; Hagar needed to be respected, too. It wasn't easy keeping a pack of hormonally surging teenaged girls in check, and the Abbess needed to watch how she spoke to Hagar, that was all. Especially in front of the Maenads.

This time it had been over the Half-Shell Mary; it had disappeared long ago, when Hagar had gone back to bury it as the Abbess had ordered, which meant that the Guatemalans had taken it. This simple explanation, however, had enraged the Abbess; more and more she hated any sign that the entire forest was not under her control, and she dwelt upon it and revisited it in her mind.

"Let them have their plaster Mary—they've already *got* a chruch . . ." Hagar had started to say, when the Abbess had checked her with a clout across the jaw. (It was true, the few remaining Guatemalans did have a stone-and-daub chapel, just a small, crude structure, roofless and open to the sky, with paneless windows and a dirt floor. But they had consecrated it with prayer and intention, and they had used it this night as they did every night, for evening prayer before sleep.)

The force of the blow dropped Hagar to one knee. "See what you've made me do!" cried the Abbess, as she scurried over to help Hagar up. Hagar pushed her away and staggered to her feet herself.

"I made you?" She shook her head. "I made you do nothing. You are losing your mind. . . what's left of it." Hagar hauled herself up and sat on the edge of the bed; it was a fact, she reflected. First, Senga, now this one.

174

She thought back to the beginning of their time in the woods, when the Abbess and she had begun to build the world of women, and she wondered that she hadn't seen it before. Yes, the Abbess had been proud, and overconfident, and . . . bossy, but they had needed someone like that, hadn't they? What would have become of them without her? Look at Senga, gibbering to herself and hiding, like a bandit; acting like everyone is out to get her . . . or Goddess help us, look at Buffy, a drooling, drunken idiot. They had needed the Abbess's drive and her ideas . . . in the beginning. But lately—Hagar had to face it, the Abbess's ideas had become more and more grotesque, and her actions more violent.

Hagar looked across at her erstwhile bedmate, who offered a smile that was all apology and artifice. A slow-growing bubble of nausea trembled and then subsided inside Hagar. "Tch, tch, tch," the Abbess chided, as if it was she who had been wronged. She held out her arms, and Hagar, swallowing hard, crawled into them.

Arms locked around each other they knelt upright together and rocked like mother and child on their bed in the candlelit gloom. The wind was picking up outside, and chips of twig and leaf were being blown against the walls of the Carousel, "tch, tch, tch"—the sounds they made a mimicry of the Abbess's clucking tongue. Hagar permitted herself to relax in the Abbess's embrace, and to allow the Abbess to stroke her hair, but she resolved to remember her anger.

The Abbess didn't know that Hagar had seen her sucking the marrow out of the cracked bones of the men and boys they killed. Hagar had seen her once and wished she hadn't; she had fled and looked no more. In the flickering candlelight, when she'd thought herself alone, the Abbess had looked to Hagar like a devil, staring up at herself and grinning in the speckled glass, her eyes bulging up from under her hairless brows in the night. Her face had gleamed with smeared fat, and almost glowed with pleasure as she cracked the bones with her teeth, and sucked and sucked like a fiend.

The Guatemalans, as they did most evenings, had retired soon after their evening prayers. There were fewer of them than there had been when the buses had first crashed, but the ones that were left slept peacefully in the open, sheltered in the space between their chapel and their gardens. White crosses marked the graves of the sisters who had died.

During their waking hours, they were as unaware as they could keep themselves from being of the things that the others in the forest did; they were pious women, they made a virtue of survival, and when the Mary statue, loosened by the small hands of the Maenads, had toppled down the wooded hill and come to rest outside their small stone chapel, the Guatemalan women had accepted it as a blessing. As they slept now, a moon-dappled night breeze kissed the statue as it stood watch over them.

As the Abbess and Hagar began to snore, some miles away Young Parry had just breached the forest, again, after leaving Old Parry to sleep off a night of hard drinking. Young Parry had tucked his father into bed and kissed his white hair, noticing as he did so that it was still plentiful on his head, and as soft as feathers, surprisingly white and soft when the rest of Old Parry was so ruddy and hard. Old Parry had taught his son to read and write, and young Parry had debated with himself the wisdom of leaving his father a note; but ultimately he'd reckoned that if all went to plan, he might be back here in Brooklyn with the girl before his father came to; he had known Old Parry to sleep for days after imbibing the Vicar's homebrew before.

As he checked his supplies at the edge of the woods, Young Parry felt happily exhilarated, and noticed with pleasure the blood pounding in his ears, and his heart thudding within his chest. He had brought with him into the forest his own and his father's electric torches, and they swung now from his belt. He also had a length of rope coiled around one shoulder, over the top of his body and under his arm, as well as a large and serviceable knife tucked into his belt, in case he had to persuade the girl quickly. But he was really hoping to persuade her without the knife or the rope or even his balled fist; he imagined perhaps she would *want* to leave the forest with him.

After all, the old women in Brooklyn were always trying to kiss and paw at him when he came to the tavern to find his father, though for his part he was sickened by their slack-jawed, toothless mouths and the stench that came off the filthy rags they wore. He knew he looked good to them, and within his mind was the barely formed thought that the girl with the red hair might think he looked good, too. Good enough to follow out of the forest. But the girl might not speak English, or speak at all, or the shock of seeing him might frighten her so much he'd have no choice but to tie her arms behind her and make her walk before him, and to do that he'd need at least to have the knife to wave at her, as a threat. He wouldn't use it. Not for cutting. Not for cutting *her*. He tightened his belt as a night breeze lifted the fringe of hair that hung over his straight, black brows, and he clicked on his father's torch as he set out under the pale moon to find his heart, the girl with the fiery hair who lived in the golden house in the forest. He remembered the way.

PART II

LEDA AND THE SWAN

A sudden blow: the great wings beating still

Above the staggering girl, her thighs caressed

By the dark webs, her nape caught in his bill,

He holds her helpless breast upon his breast.

How can those terrified vague fingers push

The feathered glory from her loosening thighs?

And how can body, laid in that white rush,

But feel the strange heart beating where it lies?

A shudder in the loins engenders there

The broken wall, the burning roof and tower

And Agamemnon dead.

Being so caught up,

So mastered by the brute blood of the air,

Did she put on his knowledge with his power

Before the indifferent beak could let her drop?

—William Butler Yeats

Chapter Twenty

The Great Wings Beating Still

AFTERWARD, THE THING NO ONE CAN EVER AGREE ON is this: was it this day or *that* that was the beginning of the end? Was it that day or *this* that was the end of the beginning? All anyone can agree on, afterward, is that there was a beginning and that there is now an end.

In the morning of the day that no one could agree on, the moon had set late and the sun rose early, pale and tired above a grey tent of clouds, sending out feeble rays that never managed to pierce the gloom. Rain teemed down throughout what had been the Greater New York area, and the forest became a sodden misery, gulleys churning and foaming with muddy rivulets, and the leaf-mold underfoot turning to slippery slime that made walking on all but the old paved roads a hazard. Buffy looked out from her lean-to and studied the curtain of rain; quickly she stripped off her threadbare bib overalls and draped them over a sopping laurel bush. Then she stood under a downspout that had formed in the v-shaped notch between the rock wall of her lean-to and the sky. She stood there naked, arms akimbo and feet planted wide apart, for long moments, shaking the water off her head and her hands every few minutes, shivering with cold and also with pleasure; it had been long since she had had a shower, and the other women balked at letting her share their baths. "It's true," she said to herself, as if someone were there to disagree with her, "a cleaning is a comfort."

Senga woke up on the now-muddy apron of grass that served the Relay Station as a back doorstep, and was momentarily confused. Why was she waking up outside, and why was it raining? Then she remembered the night before, and the argument with Pink. "Shit," she swore, and pushed herself up onto all fours before standing up, and then promptly slipped and slid wildly on the mud that had pooled as she slept. "SHIT!" she said again, and slipped again, and slowly made her way indoors. The search for Pink would have to be delayed. It wasn't as if Senga or any of the women had foul-weather gear, and the rain showed no sign of letting up. Senga would put on a kettle; her head hurt and she needed to think.

The Abbess and Hagar woke up on separate sides of the large mattress they shared in the makeshift bedchamber of the Carousel; unfortunately the vents in the Carousel's roof, so useful at times for letting smoke escape, were now admitting veritable sheets of water, and the mattress was soaked. "Shift that, will you," sniffed the Abbess, pulling her day-robe around her.

"Shift it yourself," Hagar growled, and she meant it. She wasn't ready to make up yet. She grabbed a dampish blanket and stalked off to find shelter with the Maenads in the dormitory bus. "Remember what day it is," the Abbess called after her. Hagar pretended not to hear. She knew the next Snatch would take place today, whether the rain stopped or not, and whether she helped the Abbess to prepare or not. The Maenads and Acolytes knew their roles and performed them like robots; the Abbess had trained them well. Nothing would go wrong. "I'm not needed," she thought, "and I don't care."

The Maenads, excited by the novelty of the gushing downpour, were nevertheless none-too-pleased to have Hagar force herself into their midst; quite apart from her snoring and farting, her being there meant she would commandeer a berth and two of the young girls would have to squeeze into a single bunk. They might as well get up and go outside, but the intensity of the rain made that prospect less appealing than it normally would have been.

The Guatemalans, stoic, phlegmatic, went about doing whatever it was they had planned, that day, to do. As on most

182

days, it would be something useful; if they couldn't fish, they could mend their nets. It was just rain.

In Brooklyn, Old Parry slept on, all unaware that his son had entered the forest. In boundless dreaming he was free to visit the town on the Clyde where he had been born, where the men still asked the women to dance in the same, timeworn way as their fathers had asked their mothers and their mothers' sisters:

"Are ye dancin'?"

"Are ye askin'?"

"Aye, I'm askin'"

"Then I'm dancin'"

Old Parry danced in his dreams in the arms of an impertinent girl whose family had dared to give her the dreadful, prosaic, and utterly homely name, "Agnes." In his dreams he could dance like a satyr, and the girl with the homely name felt like a sylph in his hands. He slept on long after the rain began, and long after Young Parry disappeared into the woods.

For the young ones, Yuki-Kai, Young Parry and Pink, who had walked, or wept, or whimpered for most of the night, and who might have looked forward to sleeping during this day, the rain was unwelcome, uncomfortable, and unpleasant, but nothing more. They were young and would not be deterred from their quests, even if they were wet and worn out.

Coming back to the Relay Station toward morning, Yui-Kai had spied Senga's sleeping form on the doorstep in the slowly lightening gloom, before the rain came bucketing down, and surmised that something was wrong. Creeping closer she paused only long enough to see the rising and falling of Senga's chest, assuring herself that the older woman was alive, before slinking through the half-open back door of the station. Once inside that familiar, homey place, she quickly sensed that Pink wasn't there—the station felt lifeless. At least it was devoid of the one Yuki sought. So, with many nervous glances over her shoulder toward the sleeping figure on the doorstep before Senga could wake up, Yuki snatched an apple from a bowl that was there and moved through the empty spaces toward the front door.

She paused before the entrance to Pink's bedchamber and thought about the things she had seen inside; things that could be useful in the rainy forest. The pale sun was only just rising, and by its wan light she could begin to make out, as her eyes adjusted, the blurred outlines of entryways and obstacles in the gloaming. Here was the bedroom where Pink had slept, further on the kitchen. There were matches in the kitchen, Yuki-Kai remembered, as well as some candles, and string.

She remembered a box on a high shelf in the kitchen, too, with whose contents Pink had once sought to impress her. A thing like a knife without a haft, and another thing, like a metal ball with a handle attached to a ring. "Senga hid them," Pink had said. "they're dangerous." Yuki-kai had shrugged. "She doesn't know I know." Yuki had feigned disinterest then, but the thought occurred to her now that these dangerous

184

items might be useful, although she didn't know what they were nor how they were intended to be used. But dangerous things would be better off in her and Pink's hands than lying around where Senga or the Abbess could get them. This was, in fact, the same reasoning that had led Senga to stash the hand grenade and the bayonet in the Relay Station when she had first found them years ago.

Yuki was considering how best to carry these items away with her when she realized she was not alone.

A second later, a wet and wiry hand had clamped itself onto Yuki's shoulder from behind. "Here, you," said a stern voice. Senga's.

Any thought of resistance was shaken off by the tightening of those wiry fingers. Senga turned Yuki around bodily to face her. "If you're looking for Pink, she's gone; she ran away last night," Senga said. Yuki-Kai began to reply, but Senga cut her off. "I know you fought. I know . . . . I know."

The easy acceptance with which Senga seemed to understand everything there was to understand shook the unshakeable Yuki-Kai. Senga's grip on Yuki's shoulder softened, but she made up for it by doubling her hold on the girl, placing one hand on each of Yuki's malnourished biceps. "I know" was all she said, and all she needed to say. And then the untameable, unmothered Yuki moved into the circle of Senga's arms and placed her wild head on Senga's still ample, though no-longer magnificent, breast. She wept, and Senga petted her wet hair. "You're cold," Senga told her, and Yuki

185

nodded miserably. "You're hungry, as well," she said, and Yuki agreed. "Well we won't lose very much time by having something to eat, like civilized people. Sit. She may come back on her own, caught out in this weather." Senga moved them both toward the kitchen, and indicated a stool.

"Where do you think she went?" she asked the suddenly pliable and complaisant child, Yuki-Kai, who sucked her lower lip.

Senga sighed.

"Where would *you* go?" she asked.

Yuki made a wry face and raised both her shoulders. "There aren't really that many places *to* go," said the girl, speaking directly to Senga for the first time.

Senga nodded. She began to bustle around the kitchen. She felt odd. This was so . . . ordinary, like a scene from her own childhood. Except . . . Senga thought suddenly of Grandma Mosher, who'd lived next door to them in the apartment house on Parsons Blvd. Grandma Mosher—whose grandson Steven had played *Fur Elise, on the piano,* and whose sweet face, with its collapsing, ancient cheeks that were as soft as baby roses Senga loved, and whom a lustrous, sugary, powdery scent always seemed to surround. Senga had always been thrilled to be invited into the Mosher family's clean, warm kitchen, to eat stewed fruit from a tiny, cut-glass bowl, with a silver spoon that had come, Grandma had said, from her own mother's house in *Leopoldstadt,* wherever that was. Senga shook her head to clear it.

186

She drew a wooden safety match from a box, lit it, and tossed it into the oven, and Yuki's eyes widened. Senga had almost forgotten what a luxury it was to have this shelter, the solid Relay Station, and the means with which to easily heat it. "Bring your stool closer," she instructed Yuki, "and get your wet clothes off."

None of the Maenads, especially not the bold Yuki-Kai, had any shame about nakedness. And so she stripped off, staying close to the open oven door for warmth, as Senga sped through the rooms of the Relay Station, gathering spare clothes for Yuki-Kai and other things she thought they might need. When her arms were full, she returned to the kitchen, and dumped all on the table. She cracked some eggs into a metal pan and stuck it into the oven, before flinging some of Pink's dry clothing at Yuki, who was hopping up and down in front of the oven door for warmth.

"Aaah," cried Yuki, aghast, reaching for the pan with the eggs in it. "Why did you do that?"

"I'm cooking them," Senga replied. "What did you think I was going to do with them?"

"We just usually suck them."

"I see." Senga, furrowing her brow, dropped her gaze, then raised it. "I like them cooked," she stated.

Yuki hopped on one leg as she struggled into Pink's things.

"What's that on your leg?" Senga scowled.

"Nothing. I . . . Buffy did it. Some of the other girls

have them . . . ."

Senga gripped Yuki's legs and held them apart. Above the knee, on the inner part, each of her thighs was embellished with an elaborate tattoo. Sweet-looking traceries of vines and buds at the knee grew thicker and thornier as they made their way up the inside of Yuki's legs, giving way to a tangled, thorny mass of inky briars that guarded the entrance to her body. Senga, crouching, studied each leg silently. Then she whistled. "This took some time."

Yuki nodded.

"It must've hurt."

Yuki shrugged.

"Anyway, finish getting dressed, and eat these eggs." Senga let go of Yuki's knees slowly, then stood and pulled the pan out of the oven and handed Yuki a fork. "Things have changed. You eat. We have to talk."

Miles away, Pink was waking up in the woods, drenched, and shivering, and alone. "Ugh." She realized she would have to tuck tail and return home to Senga if she didn't want to catch wet death. "Bother," she huffed, as, pulling her wet shift around her and wiping her hair off her face, she turned to face the direction she thought she'd come from the night before, which is often a mistake made by the inattentive and inexperienced, and lost.

Chapter Twenty-One

Old Parry, Young Parry

O LD PARRY CAME TO FROM HIS DRUNKEN DREAMS TO the certain knowledge that his son had gone into the forest.

The old man made his way to the bathroom and threw up; he was a seasoned campaigner, he could do it almost as an act of will, without all the retching and moaning of the inexperienced boozer. It was a part of his morning routine, and had been for many years. Raking his fingers upwards alongside his dorsal flank, he scratched himself and cleared his throat. His white hair stood up from his head and he patted it down with shaking fingers. He looked around for his tobacco and his pipe; he would have preferred to roll a smoke but he had run out of rolling paper days ago. The idea that his son might have gone out to trade for some brightened his morning momentarily, but no, Young Parry was gone. Old Parry just knew it. The house had that decidedly abandoned feel; small as it was, it echoed this morning.

It had been a find, this squat of theirs, and Parry would be sorry to lose it, but he knew his duty. If that daft boy had gone into the forest, it was up to his father to get him back out. But first things first. A curer. A smoke and a curer were needed, and with much trembling, Parry managed to fill his old clay pipe and light it, and he held it between his teeth, drawing on it while he looked, under furniture and on shelves, for the last of the whisky he'd brought home last night. The bottles clinked discouragingly until his scrabbling fingers lit upon one that still contained some pale golden fluid. "*Uisge beatha,*" he beamed, "Water of Life." He shuddered it down, pulling his thin lips thinner over his white teeth, as if in pain, as he did so.

The whisky stayed down, so he set about leaving the house in readiness for the next squatter. It was the way things were done in Brooklyn. No house was entirely whole, and none had had power or plumbing for decades, but the facilities for plumbing still snaked their ways through the walls and foundations, and there were ways to use them. Parry clenched the stump of his pipe in his teeth as he carried buckets of water from the alley that ran across the back of the building into the house. They were always kept filled, but had been topped up to brimming by this morning's rain. When he got them upstairs, he heaved them one by one onto his shoulder and emptied them into the toilet he had just used. In Brooklyn, a squatter who left his filth behind was no better than an animal, and anyone who did eventually found himself barred from even the rudest of squats.

Old vagabond Parry had just a few possessions, and so to pack up and leave a place, any place, was always a simple matter of moments, but today he spent several vexing minutes searching for his electric torch before admitting to himself that his son must have taken it. "Shite," he swore, and gave one last look around, then closed the door behind him. Stepping out into the rain, he whipped a flat tweed cap out of one of the pockets of his coat and slapped it firmly onto his head, but not before a gigantic raindrop had landed, splash, on his pink pate, finding its way down his neck and inside the back of his shirt, making him shiver. "Shite," he said again, and adjusted his bag and set off down the road toward the place were he thought his son would have been likely to enter the forest, by the remains of the old elevated train tracks that had run along Jamaica Avenue.

Parry was right; he knew his son's mind well; knew what his son would do and say on many subjects without having to ask him. Father and son not only resembled each other in looks, but in mind, and back in the days before he'd had a wife, or a son, and when he, himself had been young,

191

Parry had been called "a romantic." He'd never quite understood what a woman meant when she described him with that word, and it was probably too late to bother about it now. One woman had said he was "sensitive," while wrapped in his arms and running her fingers through his fine, dark, hair. One said he was "such a good lover," while similarly engaged. But another had called him "extremist," and said he took things too seriously when he'd asked her to marry him the first time they met. "Whatever I am, he's my spit *and* image," Parry said to himself, as he walked through the windy drizzle, approaching the edge of the forest. "And the daft boy that he *is* is in there, and after a female, I'll be bound. Nothing else makes sense."

After a female Young Parry was, and in fact, he had found her, although he didn't realize it for some moments. He had walked through the night, only using his torch at need, walking into the blackness in the direction where he thought he remembered seeing her. Some good luck was with him, because that's exactly what he *was* doing, walking toward her through the velvet darkness, and then through both darkness and rain, slipping in the mud and pulling himself up by grasping branches and vines, and always making his way toward the memory of a house of yellow brick with a red tile roof.

She was sitting on her heels, rocking and crying and looking decidedly unlike the siren of red-gold hair and rose-pink cheeks with the high, proud bosom and the fine, rounded

192

limbs who had captured him weeks ago. This girl was pale, and scrawny, and her inadequate, wet shift clung to her slender frame like a shroud, showing off not her mounded bosom but her shriveled, pointed nipples and her mud-streaked gooseflesh. That girl had had a halo of gold, red, auburn, and straw-colored curls; this creature had something dark, and wet and lank stuck to her head, that drooped and dripped down onto her shoulders and hung across her upper back like nothing so much as a string of rats' tails. Was it even a girl? Young Parry wondered, when suddenly she saw him, and screamed. "That's a girl." he thought. He'd known enough women and girls to know that was one of the main sounds they made.

As his son had been trying to figure out how to approach the wet girl, Old Parry was approaching the edge of the forest. It was marked by a naked chain-link fence that was twisted and barely standing; however that wasn't what kept people like himself out of the forest. No one could see how it was accomplished, and yet everyone had experienced it; the forest itself kept them out. But not this day. Old Parry walked up to the fence where it sagged outward and pulled down on it as his son had done hours before. He swallowed a lungful of air, and set his lips in a tight line, and stepped over the fencing—and the trees at the edge of the woods let him pass.

Chapter Twenty-Two

The Care and Feeding of Yuki Kai

"**D**ID YOU GET ENOUGH TO EAT?"

Yuki nodded, but her eyes darted to the shelf above the oven where the eggs lived.

"I could make you another egg, if you're still hungry," Senga offered.

"I'd like another egg," Yuki nodded her head. "But you don't have to cook it."

Senga handed her the egg and turned away; it wasn't that she had never sucked an egg herself, but watching someone else do it made her guts rise. She busied herself separating the items she had collected into two piles, and

194

stacking them each on the table. One for herself to carry, one for Yuki.

"Will you help me find Pink?" she asked the girl.

Yuki nodded yes.

"When I find her, she and I are leaving the forest."

"No one can leave the forest . . ."Yuki started to say, but Senga stopped her with a finger across her lips, and a look that said, *did you hear that?* Yuki shook her head, no, truthfully. Senga continued.

"Yes," she whispered, "there is a way. I've been working on it for a long time—we could have used it before, but I got lazy, and frightened."

"Frightened of what?" bold Yuki, who had been born in the forest, and knew no other world, asked. "What's there to be afraid of? Anyway, where would you go? There's nothing out there . . ."

"Oh, child," said Senga shaking her head. If the forest wouldn't let them out, they might have to escape through the last tunnel, and. . . should she explain to this fearless child about the cave-in that had buried her playmate alive, how the candles had guttered and then blown out completely, and the darkness come down like a shroud? How she had had to dig the child Pink out, grabbing fistfuls of the living dirt she was terrified to touch? Only her mother-love for Pink had sustained her, only her need for the living child had strengthened her will to plunge into the treacherous, verminous earth to rescue her foster daughter. And even if she could do that, how could she explain what the world had been like to this child who knew only the woods?

"Yes," she said, finally, "there is. I was born there. I think it's still there. I think the forest comes to an end somewhere around the cemetery fields," she gestured vaguely out the front door of the Relay Station.

"That's the Forbidden Zone!"

"Is that what they call it?" Senga laughed grimly.

"Uh-huh." Senga handed a gathering bag to Yuki, and took one for herself. Slinging them across their chests, they began stuffing the bags with the articles piled on the table.

Senga snorted. "Well, good. If it's forbidden, maybe it'll keep them out. I don't want them following us. No matter what we find out there, it'll be better to face it without these crazy bitches."

"We're not supposed to use that word, either" Yuki said. Senga arched an eyebrow at the girl.

"Oh. Do you always do what you're supposed to do?"

Yuki reached down and rubbed her leg; the Abbess's last beating still hurt a bit. "No," she smiled grimly.

Senga grinned at her and thought, *Man, they really stick to those rules.*

"I didn't think so. Hurry up.. If Pink is out there in this, she's probably frozen. The sooner we get to her the better. I can't nurse her through pneumonia; she won't make it. Her chest is weak. You can come with us or not, but we're not coming back here."

196

"I don't think they'll follow us . . . they don't like you, and they don't like me, either . . . and even if they miss us, they'll probably just think we fell into one of Buffy's traps."

"Wouldn't they expect to find our bodies there the next time they went to check?"

Yuki shrugged. "Maybe they'd think we got eaten by something."

"Bones. They'd expect to find 'em. Anyway, I'm due to deliver a big box of supplies for the next Snatch, today. They'll notice if they don't get it, and they'll come after me, at least. Look. I don't wanna talk you into anything. You can stay here if you want to. You can have this place. Seems like you know your way around here already . . . ."

Yuki looked around. She was tempted. There was much to explore here, and if Senga had kept the secret of Pink here from everyone but her, then it was a place where Yuki could also hide. But she wasn't the hiding type, and as soon as she had thought that thought, she knew she would go with Senga.

"If you won't leave with us, if you want to stay here, okay. But you have to promise not to raise the alarm. You have to let us get away. If not, if they catch us, I swear to the Goddess, I will get away from them and I will kill you, as sure as shit."

But no, if Pink was going, Yuki would go, too. She would go if it meant her death in the world of whatever was out there.

"Count me in," she said.

CHAPTER TWENTY-THREE

BLOOD AND SPECTACLE

THE RITUAL OF THE SNATCH HAD GROWN FROM A scrawny sapling with its puny roots in the earth of bare necessity to a brobdignagian growth of monstrous proportions. Every year, the Abbess added elements to the spectacle. Every year, there were more young women eligible to ride, and that meant there had to be a system in place to ensure that everyone who had started to bleed got a chance to do so, every cycle. "Waste not, want not," said the Abbess.

One year the Abbess's "system" had taken the form of a footrace, with the four nubile Maenads of the month dressed in filmy, one-shouldered scraps that fluttered down to around the tops of their thighs and were designed to facilitate easy congress with the captured men. When this paled after several months, a gladiatorial-style competition was instituted; this worked well during periods when only one captive was available for riding; the competition added an element of suspense to the goings-on, and Buffy made a small fortune running a bookmaking operation. Of course, since the women had no monetary system, the "fortune" was largely a fiction, but Buffy liked being able to brag about her ability to pick a winner.

For the last several years, the Snatch had been preceded by a pageant, written by the Abbess, narrated by the Abbess, and starring the Abbess, with various Acolytes and Maenads who had not yet begun to bleed enacting the roles of the Riders and the Ridees. Tiny, ratlike Mia was usually called upon to play the "Fruits of the Riding" in this spectacle, largely because the role called for an actress small enough to be hoisted above the stage by the same squeaking pulley and rope system that the women had used to get Putty Hair and Deeper Voice out of the pit so many years before. Frightened Mia had to hang there, squeaking and shrieking along with the rusty pulley, while below her the assembled women sang the song the Abbess had written for the first Moon Meeting so many years ago, the song Buffy had first sung, to a tune something like "Blueberry Hill,"

It's catch, before kill,

Cause a girl needs a thrill,

We must get our fill,

And don't let any spill!

Two of the sturdier Meanads would be called upon to play the roles of the ill-fated Putty Hair and Deeper Voice, wearing badly fitting, tied-on phalluses made of some kind of papier-maché, and rather-more-badly fitting wigs, and an assortment of costumery that varied from production to production, depending on what Senga could find while scavenging.

Sometimes the costumes were rather good, as they were in the years after Senga had plundered the ruins of a dental supply house—sets of dentures that had been made for patients long-dead were inserted into the mouths of the girls playing the unlucky men. They felt painful, looked hideous, and impeded articulate speech, but fortunately the men's lines were supposed to be in the nature of animal screams and grunts, and in every telling of the tale, Putty Hair and Deeper Voice were described as more and more bestial, so the worse the teeth looked, the better the characterization.

Senga had never taken an active part in the Snatch after that first time when she helped Skye slip into the cage with Deeper Voice to conceive the Maenad named Nova— who was now old enough to ride, herself. But she traded with the women who did, of course, providing them with props for the pageantry, and sometimes hanging around long enough to watch.

She stood on the doorstep of the Relay Station now with Yuki as they laid whatever plan they could in such haste.

"Meet me back here tonight no matter what; one of us is bound to find her, but if we don't, she may have sense enough to come back here herself." Into Senga's mind flashed an image of herself in a housewifely scene from the World Before. She saw herself as if she were buttoning her daughter into a raincoat and handing her a sack lunch. Only there were no housewives, no raincoats, and no lunches in this world. She wiped off a piece of eggshell that was stuck to Yuki's face. There was something about the girl that brought out long-buried feelings in Senga; not even for Pink had she felt anything like this, in many a year. A conspiratorial smile lit Yuki's thin features.

"I'll go toward Guatemala," said Senga, who wanted to take the measure of the women there. If there was a chance of violence—and with the Abbess and Hagar there was always the chance of violence—she thought she owed the Guatemalans a warning. And she could use allies in the forest in case the Outside proved unlivable. They might all have to come back.

"And I'll cover the ground between here and Buffy's."

"It's unlikely she'll have gone toward the Carousel . . . ." Senga didn't need to complete the thought.

They would all have a chance to escape while The Abbess and the others were occupied with the Snatch. Escape would bring its own terrors; the darkness of the tunnels Senga richly remembered—but unless the forest was in the mood to let them escape, the tunnels and whatever they contained would have to be braved. If the forest wouldn't let them out, Senga knew what would have to be done.

"If I don't make it back, I expect I'll end up in the stew-pots," Senga mused aloud. She cupped Yuki's cheek. "I think you and Pink should try to escape even if I don't make it. Pink can show you the way through the Relay Station and down to the tunnel if you can't get out any other way. You'll need candles, and you'll need to be brave, but I wouldn't want you to come back here. The World Outside can't be worse than this. I'm sorry I didn't go sooner. I should have been braver, but I think I was as brave as I could be at the time." Yuki nodded agreement. The memory of that last time in the tunnel made Senga shiver.

That last time Senga had dug with Pink, the time *after* the cave-in that nearly buried both of them alive, when they had had to screw up all their courage to return to the dark, they had almost gotten through. They would have, too, if . . . . Senga shuddered. *No sense scaring myself now with what might have to be done later.*

Senga had always believed that her tunnel, if she could finish it, would carry her out along the north-eastern edge of the woods, where the buses had been driving that last day, along Union Turnpike, above the old subway tracks; the E and F lines, they were called. She thought if she could just dig far enough she would find a way to break through into the man-made, well ventilated tunnels of the New York City Subway System, and from there she believed she had a chance to find her way toward something like home.

Now as she watched Yuki bounding off like a deer along the path that led to Buffy's, Senga felt fear, but she also felt vigor, and the stirring of long-deferred hope. She shifted her shoulder bag to a spot higher on her shoulder, and set off for Guatemala. The two hand grenades clanked against the bayonet, and she stopped to separate them. She would give them to the Guatemalan leader, the one her followers called *la Madre*. Beyond that, she couldn't think, but maybe she would be caught, and she didn't want those weapons to fall into the hands of the Abbess or Hagar. *In fact,* she smiled grimly as she told herself, *there's almost no chance I'll get through. But if I stay here, I'm dead anyway. I just didn't see it before.*

CHAPTER TWENTY-FOUR

CROSS PURPOSES

A S IF IT HAD BEEN TURNED OFF, THE RAIN STOPPED. However, the wet branches and drooping leaves of the woods continued to drip water, even as a ferocious sun broke through the clouds with a vengeance. As if determined to assert its rights, the heat of it made the forest steam. Pools of sunlight were reflected in the shining water-meadows and mud puddles that had appeared in the forest's numerous clearings as a result of the cloudburst.

Pink saw young Parry a moment before he saw her, and the sight of each other shocked them both into momentary paralysis. For his part, he had been looking for *his* Pink, his golden siren-girl with the freckle-spangled, rosy skin and the massy copper-colored hair—not this bedraggled urchin with the grime-streaked face and lank, wet coils of blackish twine plastered to her skull and hanging like rat-tails down her back.

For her part, it was as if she had seen a faun, or a dinosaur, or something else from one of the long-ago picture books Senga had brought her—a mythological creature, a demon, a something-that-couldn't-exist. She screamed—and he did what anyone else in his position would do—he tried to stop her.

Lunging toward her and closing the space between them in one leap, he clapped his left hand over her mouth, and with the right he brandished the knife he had intended not to use. Backing away from his advance, she was blocked by a tree at her back. This only caused her to scream harder against his muffling hand, and struggle away from him with widening, panicked eyes; he was forced to drop the knife entirely in order to subdue her with both hands, all the while repeating "Shut up, shut up, shut up!" And eventually, she would. The dropped knife buried itself up to its hilt in the earth.

There was nothing else Young Parry could think of to do but keep tight hold of the drowned-lizard girl, until she got tired of screaming, for as long as it would take. Maybe she knew where that other one was. . . . He looked around; he didn't know what for, and all the while Pink twisted and struggled and hopped from leg to leg, trying to kick him and once or twice succeeding. But his grip never loosened, although they were both wet and slippery; he was strong.

Ultimately, the wet night Pink had spent outdoors, the argument with Senga, and Yuki's thumbnail-scratch between her legs, which was beginning to throb, caused her to weary much sooner than she might otherwise have done. As soon as Parry felt her relaxing under his grip, he loosened it and whispered, "Friend. I'm a friend." Gripping her wet face to keep the hand across her mouth in place, he took the other from around her and pointed to himself, and hoped she spoke English. She jerked her head to indicate compliance, and seemed to acquiesce, and when his grip relaxed, she bit into whatever she could find of his fingers. Her fine white teeth met in the fleshy part of his index finger; as he pulled his hand away, she began to scream once more, as did he.

Young Parry shook his injured hand and stomped around, bending over double and cursing, allowing Pink time to retreat to a crevice behind a rock. She was panting, and frightened, but she wanted a better look at him. Because as startled as she had been, she was also aroused. She didn't know that's what she was, but she was. She looked around and grabbed a fallen branch to use in case he got too close.

"Are you one of *them?*"

"One of who?" He shouted, and looked around. "CHRIST!"

Here Pink was at a loss. Who, indeed? What were they called, the ones Yuki had told her about, the ones the women caught, and rode, and killed, and ate?

"Men. . .?" she ventured.

He didn't hear her.

"*Shit!*"

He held his good hand against his body, tucked into his armpit, as he shook the bitten hand and sucked his teeth.

"OW! Son of a bitch!" Shaking the hand didn't help; he clutched it to his shirt-front, where a rose of blood began blossoming, alarmingly quickly.

Pink stared at him, like an owl. There seemed to be no rejoinder to this, and so she made none.

But after he swore and stamped and shook his hand some more, she became irritated.

"I didn't even bite you that hard. Anyway, I asked you a question: did you escape?"

"You did too bite hard, and I heard you, and I don't know what you're talking about—I didn't escape, I just walked up to the trees and . . . they just let me in, like last

208

time." He held out his hand and showed her his slick, red, spurting finger. It dripped with gore. Pink had enough sense in her to hide her pleased surprise. She put on a sad expression.

"Sorry," she offered, and shrugged. "Maybe you have thin skin."

"You fucking BIT me! And I didn't escape from anyone; I came here to look for someone!"

What the man-thing was saying made no sense, but Pink had had no experience with conversation, or with much of anything, so the idea that she and the man, *if* he were a man, were talking at cross-purposes would not have occurred to her. What did occur to her was how fine he looked, with his fierce, straight, slanting brows, and his blue eyes with their black lashes, and the shiny black shock of hair that fell over his right eye. His cheeks were flushed under their high cheekbones, not with drink, like his father's, but with exertion, and youth, and the pain in his hand where she'd bitten him. She tried again, speaking slowly, as Senga had to her when she was small and Senga was trying to explain something complicated and important.

"Are . . . you . . . what . . . they . . . call . . . a . . . man?"

"Are you kidding?"

"I don't know 'kidding'. I think you might be a man, and if you're a man, you must have escaped from *them—*

because men aren't allowed to just walk around wherever they want. So. . . ARE you a man?"

This little lizard of a girl must be crazy. The sun was warming her hair, and while it couldn't do anything about the streaks of dirt on her face, it was rapidly drying the ropy tangle of twine on her head. She didn't look quite so bad as she had at first. Not like his siren, but maybe like her sister, if she had one.

"Look, I don't know what you're talking about, but in Brooklyn, men are allowed to do whatever they want, and I walked here from Brooklyn, and it wasn't that far, it's all, like, joined-on, so it seems to me that the same rules that go for Brooklyn, go for here. Anyway, who's to stop me? *You?*" At that his hand gave a twinge, and he hoped she wouldn't notice the absurdity of his taunt.

And as he was speaking and thinking and twingeing, Parry stared—this girl was changing before him into something very like the girl he had braved the forest to find. Could they all do that here? Maybe there was only one girl, and she just looked different at different times. That might be a good thing, and then again it might not. The sun was drying her hair and her clothing; she looked less like a shivering monkey and more like the creamy pink creature of Young Parry's quest.

"What's your name?" she shouted, poking her tree limb at him; it was stout, which was desirable in a weapon, but heavy, and she'd been brandishing it at him for several minutes now. The muscles in her arms, unused to the exertion, were beginning to tremble. Young Parry noticed.

"It helps if you hold it on your shoulder, like a baseball bat," he said. Pink frowned. Should she accept his help? Was this a trick? Almost unconsciously, she shifted the branch.

"A *what* bat?"

"Baseball . . . you know . . ." and he mimicked a player batting a ball. She shook her head.

"I know 'bats.' We have bats here, but they're . . . animals. They fly around, and they get in your hair. They live in tunnels in the ground" (she shuddered) "and they fly out at night to eat bugs."

So it seemed that Pink and this other young person could speak each other's language, but that they still had some difficulty understanding each other. If only she hadn't parted so badly from Senga; she needed to ask her about this. That's it; she would have to go back. She sighed.

"You," she called to him, shifting the branch so that it rested on her shoulder "what's your name?"

"Parry," he said. "What's yours?"

"Pink."

Chapter Twenty-Five
Like Riding a Bike

FOR THE FIRST TIME IN MORE THAN A QUARTER-CENTURY, Senga dozed next to Parry. After their long separation and their strange meeting, they had kissed, and argued, and wept. Emotional, stunned, and shocked, they had worn themselves out with questions and answers, and then they curled into each other and slept like lost children in the woods.

She listened for a few moments to his light snoring, and smiled to herself. He turned toward her, onto his back; he was waking, but slowly. She would help him.

She turned onto her side to face him, and ran her hand over the still-taut drum of his abdomen. The hairs that downed it were numerous and grey, but they were fine and soft under her hand. He gave a sharp snort but remained asleep as her hand traveled down to the place where his body ended and what she was looking for began. She found it.

It was stout, and hard, and lying upright against his belly. She stroked it and let it move in her hand. "*Like ridin' a bike*," she thought to herself, and wrapped her hand around it so that with the soft webbing between her thumb and fingers she could gently peel back the velvet cloak of his foreskin. She sucked once, then placed one hand on the ground on either side of him, and pushed herself up lightly to get one leg over him. Perching above him, one knee on either side of his massive thighs and her head at the level of his cock, she firmly, but gently kept him down with one hand pressed against his solar plexus. Lowering her head, she looked up at him from under her eyebrows, and took him into her mouth, and sucked on the thing that was softest and hardest at once, until he gave a muffled growl.

"Eh, lass." He looked down at her briefly, then put his head back on his earthen pillow and smiled. She smiled, too.

214

"Be still," she whispered, "and know that I am God,"

He made a soft, snorting laugh, but did as she said.

She closed her eyes then, and plied him with her tongue; and savored the taste she hadn't tasted in too many years. The indescribable, gamey, salty, goaty, man-taste, the same as she remembered—and just as she remembered, it filled her mouth and nose with the iron smell of his living blood. The head of his cock was smooth and slick, and the organ itself pulsed muscular and round against her tongue, and she was close to losing herself in her play, when he pushed her off gently, afraid he wouldn't last long enough in her mouth to get a chance to feel her soft insides, her body's velvet walls that were as slick as glass and hotter than hot. He turned her around to face him and laid her down, and as he slid into her she took him with a self-satisfied grunt.

"Yes, you are," he looked into her eyes, and answered. "And I am your fervent disciple."

It had happened like this—after parting from Yuki-Kai, Senga had made her way down toward Kettledrum Hill; it was the last place she and Pink had been together (had it been only yesterday morning?), and for that reason alone she had hoped she might find the girl there. She had looked along the path the Maenads had taken, she noted the jagged stump where triumphant Yuki-Kai had held aloft the snake, she beat down the ferny undergrowth, but she saw no sign of Pink, for

215

Pink wasn't there. Instead, Senga found the last person in the world she had thought she would ever see again: it was a man, and not only "A" man, it was "THE" man. Her man. It was her old Parry. She shook her head, but he was still there when she blinked with her good eye and looked again.

The last time she had seen him he had been putting her on one of the buses that were waiting in parking lot E of the Queens College campus, in the early dark of a May morning in 1972. *How long ago? Twenty years, thirty, or more?* He hadn't been her only boyfriend, but he was the only one who could be counted on to see her off on a trip.

"Be careful," he'd said, and kissed her.

"I will," she'd said, and kissed back.

She'd watched him out the window as she took her seat, curling her fingers and giving a little wave, as he'd ridden off on his bike to his job at a drugstore in Brooklyn. She'd spent some moments settling into the leather seat with its aroma of luxury that the "executive-sized," hired, tourist-coach provided. They were driving along Union Turnpike and had just passed over Queens Boulevard—with its mayor-banished landmark of public statuary, "Civic Virtue," an inartistic, burly, naked young man made of marble and wielding a sword, astride two voluptuous marble women—when the first temblor hit. The actual young women on the buses, buoyant with purpose and fervor to advance their

216

worthy cause, ignored it if they felt it at all. It had been cold that day, Senga remembered, but fair; the sun was not quite up; it was a six-hour drive to Washington from Queens and they were leaving early to arrive in good time. Parry had a long ride in front of him, but he was hours early.

The bus driver was winding the handle of the destination sign in the front window to read "Washington, D.C." The signs and banners the women had painted in the days before the trip and brought with them were stowed in the luggage bins beneath the bus; it was only to be a day trip so there had been no need to pack many clothes. The "non-perishable canned foods" they were bringing—donations for the needy as their price of admission to the demonstration—filled the spaces not taken up by the banners. Some of the non-perishable goods, notably the ones Buffy stowed—and with comically elaborate, and inept, surreptitiousness—stowed after everyone else had taken her turn, clinked and clattered. Buffy was being so careful with them, Senga remembered; they were only canned goods, were they not? She had laughed. Inside, both buses were loud with the noises of young women, and high spirits, and hope.

As they rumbled past the beefy and unsubtle work of public art, Senga's seatmate, who, had she known she had only moments to live, might have said something different, sneered, "*That's* typical . . . *man,* the virtuous, trampling women, who, of course, represent vice and sin!" The pretty, prim, bespectacled, soon-to-die blonde wore braids under a kerchief, Senga had noted, and had tiny marks on her even, regular teeth where her braces had recently been. Senga shrugged at her and smiled. "We'll change all that someday, won't we?"

The driver had just made the lane change that would take them onto the Interboro Parkway when chaos erupted into the world. They had thought it was just a rough patch of road, or a sideswiping accident at first, but it had built on itself and grown louder and darker and more and more immense. It tumbled them over and over until they had come to a stop just inside the eaves of Forest Park. And the women who lived had been shaken and shocked, and battered and broken and bruised, and no one had come to help. They had had to help themselves. Or die. The forest had begun to come alive, and all around the world, a rough magic broke through and took hold, and this morning it seemed to be taking matters into its own hands, again.

In the now, Senga had been about to turn back, to return to the Station to wait for Yuki at as they had planned, when she saw him. She had delivered the weapons to the one called *La Madre*, and explained to that woman what she intended to do. *La Madre* whistled as she felt the weight of the bag Senga handed her, and placed her free hand on Senga's shoulder in blessing. "*Vaya con dios, amiga mia*" she told her.

"*Vaya con dios*, you, too," Senga answered, and began the slow, uphill walk back to the Station; neither *La Madre* nor any of the other Guatemalans had seen a young girl that day, and Senga retraced her steps desultorily. The ferny patch. Yuki's Stump. Kettledrum Hill . . . .

And then she saw him.

Of course, she thought, *this is it: I've finally gone mad. Really mad.* She peered and squinted at him, or it, while trying not to disclose her position; if he was real, he hadn't seen her yet.

He looked like he'd been sleeping rough, which of course he had—but it would have taken more than a bad night after a twenty- or thirty-odd-year-long separation to make her forget what he looked like. Of course, he had changed and aged, and it was that which decided her that he wasn't a mere vision; the man she was looking at was the same age as her. Surely in her imagination, he'd be younger?

His hair, what she could see of it under his flat cap, was wet and looked dark, as dark as it had been the last time she'd seen him in life. His skin still looked like some ruddy bark, and his eyes were still a piercing blue above his high-boned cheeks. She smiled; the gin blossoms still didn't look half bad on him—she'd always thought they gave a jaunty color to his cheeks.

Undecided yet as to whether or not she'd gone mad, she put her hand up to rub her eyes, and felt the edges of the patch that covered the ruined socket where her left eye had been; and she suddenly felt self-conscious. She suddenly felt like a woman.

The man, for of course it was Old Parry, was resting on a rock by the side of the path she had been following; a few more yards and a turn in the road and she'd have collided with him. As she watched him through the natural screen of sparsely growing saplings, it was his actions, even more than the cloth cap, the gin blossoms, or the blue eyes that convinced her he was real. It was the way his hungry hands pattered over his clothing, searching for something he needed. A cigarette, a flask.

"Come out, you," he shouted. Senga smiled. It was him, or a hallucination that sounded, looked, and acted exactly like him. *What the hell, why not answer?*

"Parry?" She reflected that she hadn't left her spot on the path—he must have sensed her rather than seen her.

"Come out!" he repeated, ignoring the use of his name.

"Come out yourself," she answered.

"Feckin' woman, have you been here all along?" He grabbed the cap off his head and twisted it in both hands. He began cautiously walking toward the sound of her voice, but sideways, like a crab, and she had to laugh.

"What do you mean all along? Where the hell have YOU been?" If this really WERE Parry, Senga knew she had nothing to fear, but lots to be annoyed at. And also a great deal to wonder over, and rejoice in. If this was her Parry, then she was safe.

Chapter Twenty-Six

Hagar on Top

Engaged as they were with each other, neither Senga nor Parry heard Hagar approach. Sleep had taken hold of them again, and they were cradled in idyllic oblivion at the side of the road, where they had surrendered to insentient bliss.

Hagar had found sleep elusive, and decided to walk; the rain, she observed, was letting up, and she still had what she called "a mad on." Her anger grew cold as she stalked through the woods, but her bitterness toward the Abbess was of long standing—easily stirred up, slow to subside. She took this most recent resentment and folded it into small squares, and tucked it away in the part of her mind marked "Enemies." It was Senga and Parry's bad luck to be spent and sleeping in each other's arms near the path Hagar had chosen that morning. She almost fell over them, and would have awakened them if she hadn't caught herself quickly and pulled back.

"Heavenly *mother,*" she whispered, "are you kidding me? This is too easy," It wouldn't have been, not if her victims had been awake and aware of her, but of course they were not. So it was only a matter of finding the right weapon and then creeping up quietly, and although she was out of practice, Hagar could still do that.

Weapons were everywhere in the woods: rocks and tree limbs for a quick battering, poisonous plants for slow torture, there were even flints for cutting, and there was always earth for stuffing into victim's mouths until they suffocated. Hagar had used each of these at one time or another, so it was the work of an instant to pick a stout branch for a prod, and a rock for a cosh. Her first blow was delivered to Parry; it was not designed to kill him, but to get his attention, once he regained his wits. Senga she had to restrain herself from killing right then and there; however, Hagar had an idea that it would be more enjoyable to draw out whatever she did now, and so when she tapped Senga's skull she did it with the measured, practiced touch of an executioner; enough to almost crack the skull at the temple, where it is weak. Senga would have a bad headache. But she would live.

Having stunned Parry, Hagar whipped off the blanket she'd had wrapped around herself and threw it over his recumbent, wounded form the same way that she and the other women threw nets over prey. It would confound him once he came to. With Senga momentarily unconscious, Hagar whistled for her most trusted Maenads; they would respond, if within earshot. Her pets were well trained. When they came scurrying up, Hagar instructed them to bind Senga's and Parry's hands. "Let them walk, but keep their hands tightly bound." She bid two of the girls to stay with her and her captives, and the rest to return to their cohort. "Not a word, though, if you know what's good for you, she threatened. "This is MY surprise." The three smallest girls dashed off, relieved to be released from duty.

The two who remained were agog at the sight of Senga, who was groggily shaking her head and propping herself up on her arms. "No woman shall strike another woman," whispered one to the other, in a small, sibilant voice, too low for Hagar to hear.

"*Without cause*," said the second Maenad, her eyes on Senga. "They added that."

The first girl nodded, eyes wide. "I guess this is the cause."

Parry was stirring; the blanket was doing its job and the Maenads made quick work of tying his hands as he struggled out of the blanket. By the time they had bound him he had shaken it off, and was looking from Hagar to Senga, enraged.

Hagar whistled to the Maenads and jerked her head towards the east. "The sunken road," was all she said. Prodded and bound, the captives had no choice, but to move ahead as their captors indicated, but Old Parry's anger was giving off a heat that Senga could feel. It was not directed at her, but if once he got the chance, it would be well not to be in its path. He had never turned the full force of his anger on her, but she had seen him fight. She hoped he still could; she intended to escape, no matter who or what stood in her way. Parry would ever be on her side; she knew that. But any hope of surreptition or stealth was gone now. It would be fighting. So be it.

CHAPTER TWENTY-SEVEN

PINK AND PARRY

"T HAT'S NOT A NAME FOR A PERSON."

"It is, too. Anyway, I asked you a question. Two questions. . . ." Pink had the branch on one shoulder now, and Young Parry's hand was dripping less and throbbing more. She noticed him wince. "Hold your arm up above your head," she ordered. He obeyed, and grinned at her. The throbbing slowed. The eager sun

226

had almost completed its drying of her hair, along with that of the clothes they were each wearing, and just as the rose of blood on young Parry's shirt had blossomed and spread, the great bloom of red-gold hair on Pink's head was beginning to reassume its massy, bewitching aspect.

Young Parry was smiling to himself in spite of his pain, because he was beginning to understand some of what he had heard his father and the other old men in Brooklyn talking about. About women, how they never gave up on an idea once they got it into their heads, and how their mouths were their weapons, how they talked and talked *all* the time—and he had already heard *this* one scream—and how beautiful they were and how changeable and dangerous they could be, but how utterly worth possessing, if you could get one to call you her own.

He didn't know this—but when he smiled he was as handsome as Pink was beautiful, with his smile that was crookedly perfect; off-center and white. When he grinned like this he had a dimple in his cheek. As Pink watched him, her hand went unbidden to her own cheek. Pink's face then grew fierce, but it also assumed a rosy, mottled blush, which spread upward 'til it disappeared in her beautiful hair. "Your name," she insisted.

"Okay, okay," he shrugged. "Parry. My full name is Royston Parry, but no one calls me Royston. Mostly they call me Young Parry, because of my father. And yes, I am what you'd call a man, I guess. A boy, really. Maybe a man. I dunno. A man. A man."

"Well okay, Royston Parry. Now everybody in this forest has just one name, and mine's Pink, and if you don't like it, that's too bad. And this isn't Brooklyn, wherever that is, and you are my prisoner. And it's a good thing for you that you are, because even though I bit you, that was just in self-defense. I won't kill you and eat you," she proclaimed. "But I may just ride you," she said, out of the side of her mouth as she had seen Yuki-Kai say things. She prodded him forward. "We'll go to my house; my mother will know what to do with you."

Now that he had heard from her lips that this forest was full of women who actually *did* kill and eat men, he believed the stories he'd heard back in Brooklyn. But it was hard to credit this delicate girl, whose beauty was blossoming every moment, as a murderer, or, worse, a cannibal. However, she *had* taken a chunk out of him already.

"Whoa, whoa, whoa," Young Parry hesitated. "Won't your mother want to kill me and eat me? And what else did you say, 'ride' me?" (What that could be young Parry had no idea.)

Pink wrinkled her nose, "Oh, Goddess, no; Senga's too old to ride anymore. Eccch!" She stuck out her tongue and her mouth formed a rictus of disgust. Young Parry blinked at her inquiringly, but she didn't explain.

"She's not like the others. They're the ones who ride and kill and eat. They hate her, and she hates them."

"Oh, good—I'm so glad you're taking me to meet someone who is probably the enemy of everyone else in this place, just as long as she won't try to eat me."

Young Parry had lost a lot of blood, and Pink pitied him, but she prodded him forward, just the same. His head was beginning to swim, and he put out his good hand to steady himself on the tree trunks that bordered the trail. "Keep an eye out for pits," Pink told him, "or you *could* end up getting eaten. And look for a yellow building with a red roof . . . that's our house, mine and Senga's. My mother's."

Something in what she said tugged at his memory, but all the talk about getting eaten drove it out.

"Pits . . . what do you mean, like peach pits?"

"I don't know 'peach pits,' I guess they're like the bats. Maybe you have different things in Brooklyn. . . "

"Yeah, I guess we do . . ."

"Pits in the ground, I mean. Like holes . . ."

"Like this?" Young Parry grabbed at a sapling and lifted his foot out of a hole in the ground which had opened up before him, and he swayed against Pink, out-of-balance as he was and already dizzy from blood loss. He grew a little dizzier, and so did she, from that swooning, swaying, gossamer touch of skin against skin. The tips of her ears grew hot and red under her mane of hair, and she cleared her throat and straightened up.

"Like that," she nodded, gravely.

"Well slow down, willya? What's the rush?"

"We can't let them catch us. They've never seen me, and I don't want them to catch me. Senga would be furious. They'd kill her; she's broken about a thousand rules. And if they catch you, they'll kill you. . .and . . . . We just need to get home to my mother."

Pink's hesitation reflected her knowledge of what would happen if Parry were found. It also reflected her urgent desire to keep him as secret as Senga had tried to keep her. The idea of his capture and death had flickered into and out of her eyes in a trice, but it was there long enough for him to catch it. However, something else in what she said puzzled him, and what he said was

"What do you mean, they've never *seen* you?"

"They've never *seen* me; I'm a secret. I hide; I've been hidden; Senga's been hiding me ever since I was born. She doesn't want them to get me; she doesn't want me to become one of them."

"Is she crazy? You can't hide a whole person!"

"I think she is a little crazy. But she's my mother, and I fought with her last night, and I ran away, and that's how you came across me back there. Now hurry up; I'm sorry your hand hurts, but you have to hurry up, or the Girl Scouts will find us; they come this way sometimes."

"If she's your mother, why do you call her Senga?"

Pink lifted her shoulders. "I dunno, that's what she taught me to call her; it's her name. Anyway, she's not my *ac*tual mother . . . *which* I just found out . . . which is one of the things we fought about. Not only did she keep *me* a secret, she kept THAT a secret from me!" As Pink held her tree branch before her, she indicated with her head the direction she wanted Parry to take. Even though she had her weapon, Parry could have subdued her. But he had finally realized that this was the girl he had come to the forest to find, and he was enjoying her company.

And so he obeyed her silent commands, and they made their way, single-file, through the woods, up the slope to where Pink thought the Relay Station should be. Her commands were silent, but—girl that she was—she was not; as they walked she told him the story Senga had told her the previous night, and they walked and they walked and when she was finished with her story, the Relay Station was in view. And Young Parry was in love.

Chapter Twenty-Eight

Surprising Buffy

BUFFY WAS SINGING; THAT'S HOW YUKI KNEW WHERE to find her. The lyrics were her own, but the melody was something of a cross between "Oh, Tannenbaum," and "Ach du Lieber, Augustine." Of course Yuki didn't know this; she had never heard recorded music, or any music other than what the Abbess's women sang or what the Guatemalans played on their pipes. Nevertheless, even her unschooled ears knew Buffy couldn't sing a lick, so when she

233

heard a tone-deaf contralto braying:

"Your tits are so adorable, bloo-bloo-bloo-bloo-bloo-bloo....

Your bits are so explorable, bloo-bloo-bloo-bloo ....

But why are you so hor-r-r-rible, bloo-bloo-bloo-bloo, to

me-e-e-e?"

she knew it had to be Buffy. Who else would be singing, or indeed doing much of anything out-of-doors, in the rain, along the booby-trapped and guarded road that led to Buffy's pot plantation-cum-distillery?

Her ablutions complete, Buffy was still singing lustily as she swung her arms and walked back to her shelter from her impromptu shower. She recognized Yuki-Kai as she approached, even before Yuki-Kai saw her. Buffy liked the wild girl and had been pleased when she had come to her for her initiation tattoo last fall. And although Hagar and the Abbess had been disappointed when any of Maenads failed to fall pregnant that season, Buffy was glad it hadn't happened that way for Yuki-Kai. Somehow she liked the idea of the lone wild girl, loose and free like herself. She couldn't imagine Yuki-Kai pregnant or nursing.

***

As Yuki walked toward Buffy, she was making up her mind that she would limit her questions to whether Buffy had seen anyone pass, or heard anything unusual that morning; but now that she was here, she began to think that wouldn't do.

She faced a choice—would Buffy be more likely to

234

help her if Yuki told her everything—everything meaning all about Pink? Yuki reasoned that if she, and Senga, and Pink were leaving the forest anyway, what difference would it make who knew about Pink? And who'd believe old stoned and loaded Buffy if she told the others the truth—that there was a free girl somewhere in the forest who belonged to Senga? Still, Yuki was political enough to understand that what Buffy didn't know, neither Hagar nor the Abbess could torture out of her. At the door of Buffy's hut, Yuki paused and called out, "Anyone at home?"

The rain had stopped completely by this time, and Buffy's arboreal shower had turned itself off altogether. Buffy wasn't in home, of course, but she was nearby, striding naked up the path toward Yuki, wringing out her wet overalls with her meaty, muscular hands as she advanced. She waved at Yuki as soon as she saw her; yes, she liked this wild girl who gave the mean Hagar so much trouble.

"Hey, Yuke." She smiled.

"Hey."

"You're . . . out . . . early," Buffy observed, slightly out of breath.

"Yeah . . . um . . . uh, I was looking for somwuh-uh-something."

Buffy began pulling her wet overalls over her damp, hairy legs, a process that took much effort. The wet, heavy denim of the trouser-legs stuck to itself, and the wet skin of Buffy's legs added friction and subtracted glide.

"What kind of somwuh- something?" she grunted. Buffy's obstinate trouser legs were taking most of her attention, but she thought she knew what Yuki wanted. A certain number of the Maenads had always been curious about Buffy's pipes and potions. Yuki was just the type, too. A little young, maybe.

With a grunt and a heave, Buffy got the bib straps over her shoulders and fastened; she would let the sun dry the garment on her body. "What the hell," she thought to herself; I was her age when I started. Probably."

Washed and dressed as she now was, she felt clean and calm and at peace with the forest and most everything in it. She was inclined to be generous.

"Let's see what we've got here." She made to enter her shelter; there was a clean pipe and some gentle weed that might do, there—but Yuki stopped her with a hand on her arm. She had decided to tell. She'd remembered that with Buffy, it was best to be explicit and direct, and so Yuki decided to tell all she knew. But slowly, a bit at a time.

"There's a girl..." she began, as Buffy sized her up. "A, a, Maenad. . . she's, ah . . . missing."

Buffy cocked her head at Yuki and pushed out her thick, liver-colored lower lip, then swallowed it with its upper partner. So it wasn't weed Yuki was after.

It was Buffy who measured her words, now. "Oh," she said. "A missing Maenad. I thought you might mean you were looking for Senga's girl." She looked as innocently as she could at Yuki-Kai, whose mouth opened in denial, or protest, or awe, or a combination of all three.

"You know about her?" Yuki remained openmouthed—too amazed to realize that she had confirmed what Buffy might only have been guessing at. Buffy nodded.

"Sure I do."

Yuki's head swam. "But . . . ."

Buffy smirked enigmatically. "Sometimes, when people think you're stupid, it's good to let them think it," she explained jovially. She jerked her head in the direction of the Carousel. "People like the Abbess, and Hagar, especially. I don't mind; I *am* kinda stupid. But Senga's okay. She doesn't hurt anyone. She's my friend, I guess. If she wants to pretend a baby is hers, and hide her from everyone else, and dig tunnels 'til she can't dig anymore, I don't mind. Why should I?"

Yuki stared for several moments at this completely unexpected version of Buffy before she remembered her errand, and how urgent it had seemed just moments ago. But by the time Yuki had recovered her composure, Buffy had lit up a pipe. She offered it to Yuki, who declined.

Buffy sat on a stump that served for a bench outside her front door, and inhaled, filling her by-now-leathery lungs. "I knew Senga from before, you know. . . ." she choked out the words as she tried to keep as much of the smoke as possible inside her chest.

Buffy's attention span was short, and her lonely

237

existence made her eager for any audience she could acquire. Yuki-Kai was impatient, but she liked Buffy, and that made her wait politely. But not for too long.

"Um, Buffy . . . ?"

But Buffy continued.

"It was Senga that gave me the name, "Buffy." Did you know that?"

Yuki was vexed. She shook her head no, and waved her hand in front of her face to disperse the pungent, sweet-smelling smoke that Buffy was exhaling. Her nose crinkled violently.

"Buffy," she started, "I need . . ." but Buffy was off. Crossing her bulky legs at the ankle, she leaned back and folded one arm behind her head. She was lost and reveling in the memory of a day in her long-ago girlhood. She, an oversized, ungainly teenaged girl with a center part in her lank, mouse-colored hair, a face full of spots, and an ill-fitting bathing suit, had inspired the quick-witted, pretty, thoughtless young Senga. It *was* true, she had looked like a large, west-African water-mammal. But until Senga, no one had been tactless or bold enough to mention it. And then Senga did, forever erasing her new friend's prosaic given name: it had been "Mary Anne."

"Yep. From then on, I was Buffy. I didn't mind. I liked it . . ."

"Buffy," Yuki finally burst. "Senga's in trouble!"

"Who. . .?"

238

Yuki grabbed the pipe. "Senga! Your friend! Who gave you your name! I need your help . . . I need you to pay attention. You can have this later." She threw the pipe down. Buffy looked innocently hurt, and her eyes scanned the ground for the pipe. But she couldn't ignore Yuki's words, which now flew out of her mouth.

"Your friend, Senga, is in trouble; you were right, it's her girl that ran away, and I need you to help me find her before the others do. And if you do that, you . . . you can come with us."

"Where to?"

"Outside the forest. We're leaving."

"Gee. I dunno . . ." Buffy looked toward the marijuana seedlings that were growing in pots she had set out on the cleared space in front of her door, the space she called her verandah.

"You don't have to come . . . but we could use your help."

And before Yuki could say another word, Buffy decided. She stood up and pushed open her front door. Entering her shelter, she took a bag off a hook made from a bent nail. From another nail she grabbed a hat—from somewhere else in the rubbishy mess underfoot she located a pair of boots (into which she jammed her large feet) and a bottle of something she took a gulp from and re-sealed with a cork. Moving more quickly than Yuki had ever seen her do, she strode to her washline and plucked a cleanish, rain-dampened rag, which she handed to Yuki, wordlessly.

More delicately than Yuki would have believed possible, Buffy's hamlike hands picked the dainty cannabis sproutlings from the tubs on the verandah where they were waiting to be transplanted into the pot field behind her house. She laid each one like a sleeping child in the rag in Yuki's hands, and then rolled the rag delicately around the lot before placing everything gently into her bag, which she slung over her shoulder.

"If Senga's not gonna be here, I don't wanna stay here anymore," she told Yuki by way of explanation. She stowed the corked bottle in her bib pocket, and crammed the floppy hat onto the back of her head.

Yuki was glad to hear it; she had thought they might need Buffy's broad back, and if she was on their side, it meant there was one less woman on the Abbess's side. If there was to be fighting, that would matter.

"Okay," Yuki said,"let's go. If you didn't see anyone or hear anything, we should head back to the Relay Station; Senga told me to meet her there whether I found Pink or not."

"Is that her name?" Buffy asked. "The girl we're looking for?"

Yuki nodded. Buffy bent over suddenly, to Yuki's alarm.

"What's wrong; are you sick?" she cried.

Then she noticed a flash of serrated steel in the sunlight, and Buffy was upright again and handing her a

240

young sapling from which she began stripping the leaves. Yuki was impressed by the speed with which Buffy had produced and used the sizeable knife. "Everyone is different today," she thought. "Things are changing."

Handing a stripped sapling to Yuki and keeping one for herself, Buffy grinned. Her sapling, a walking stick now, still had a jaunty leaf or two on top. "We've got a way to go, so let's get going." She had never been inside the Relay Station before, but she knew the way.

Chapter Twenty Nine

Naked

PINK AND PARRY HAD REACHED THE RELAY STATION IN A high state of excitement. Their youth, the danger they were in, the newness of each other, and the raw physical beauty of each in the other's eyes . . . so much combined to send the blood pumping into their loins and away from their brains. Once reason and custom were so stripped away, Pink knew the form of her desire. And Young Parry knew his, as well, as the drowned monkey-girl had become, during their almost-daylong journey through the woods, the fiery golden siren whose perfection had lured him into this strange world.

When the thick door of the Station had boomed shut

behind them, once Pink had called "Senga!" and received no reply, she and Young Parry reached for each other like drowning souls. Hearts knocking in their breasts, they began fumbling out of their thin rags. They tumbled each other to the floor, where they lay for long minutes in each other's arms, writhing and kissing with lips, teeth, and tongues—mouths open as if to devour each other, then exploring with lips gently pressed to each other's softest skin. Kiss followed kiss as with trembling fingers they searched each other's faces, absorbing each other's loveliness through their naked skin. Young Parry's injured hand, which had stopped bleeding, started again. He ignored it, but Pink took it and licked off the blood. His blood, which she had drawn. As she licked and sucked his fingers, he felt more strongly the by-now familiar, insistent heaviness between his legs. She, too, felt the weight of her sex gathering to a point between her thighs, pressing her forward to hold herself against him.

His standing member was pounding and stout with blood, and Pink too, was wet and dusky, and slick. As they dove into each other they were so intent, that, like Senga and Old Parry, earlier that same day, they never knew they were observed.

But their observers were more benign than their parents' had been.

For Buffy and Yuki had arrived at the Relay Station some moments after the young lovers, whom they glimpsed now, through the front window. Wordless and captivated, the two new friends moved closer, the better to observe the lovemaking unfolding before them. Infected by such a contagion of love, their arms crept around each other, Buffy's warm and sisterly around Yuki's thin shoulders, Yuki's around the older woman's substantial waist, and they sighed to see such love and lust so manifest and entwined before their eyes.

Yuki, who despite everything was at bottom ever a good friend, felt a soft twinge of jealousy. But she smiled inwardly to see that Pink had found her heart's true home. Buffy gave her shoulder a consoling squeeze, and Yuki smiled at her wistfully, as each of them took a long breath. A tear escaped from Yuki's eyes and she wiped it off with her wrist.

Buffy exhaled.

"I used to fuck like that," she sighed.

* * *

One hundred yards behind the watchers, unseeing and unseen by them, traveling along an overgrown, sunken path of her own discovering, Hagar passed, prodding Senga and Old Parry ahead of her. Two Maenads brought up the rear. Neither group saw the other. Both groups of women, intent on their errands, continued to do what they had been doing, oblivious to the other's presence so close by. The angry caravan passed wordlessly on its way to the Carousel Lawn.

"Let's give 'em some privacy, huh?" Buffy whispered hoarsely, and Yuki nodded in agreement. Turning their backs to the ongoing love scene unfolding beyond the window, they rested against, and then slid down the wall of the Relay

244

Station. They came to rest with their knees bent, their seats on the earth and their backs to the wall. Buffy pulled out the bottle she'd stowed in her bib, and pulled the cork.

"Want some?" she offered.

Yuki sniffed, then shrugged. "Sure."

So the two exiles drank together companionably, and Buffy told Yuki the story of how she and Senga had first met, and then lost each other, and come together again on the fateful buses. She had gotten to the part about how she had met Hagar, when the stiffness in her knees told her half-an-hour had passed.

"That's enough time for a healthy-lookin' kid like him," she announced. To Yuki she said, "Go ahead and knock on the door. They should be done, now."

And as it happened, they were done—but they had gone.

Buffy and Yuki pushed open the heavy wooden door that they had knocked on in vain; it was unlocked. Calling and calling Pink's name, for they didn't know Royston Parry's, their voices echoed off the high-ceilinged walls and bounced back at them unanswered. They looked at each other, each of them very much at a loss.

"Where could they be?" each asked the other, in unison.

"I'll look upstairs," Buffy offered, then, seeing the spindly metal spiral of steps that led to the upper floor, she thought better of it.

"On second thought, you go upstairs. I'll look around down here."

But five minutes later they were back in the front hall where Pink and Parry had abandoned themselves so beautifully not an hour ago; the Relay Station was empty. At least it was empty of human life. Of useful things it was still full. Yuki's thoughts turned to the dangerous things Pink had showed her; did Buffy know about them? She had no words for them, no names for the bayonet and the hand grenades. She couldn't ask.

The sun was slipping down the afternoon side of the sky. With a golden finger it touched the inner walls of the front hall of the relay Station with beams of light in which motes of dust danced languidly.

"It's getting late. I need to get back to the Carousel Lawn for the Snatch," Buffy told Yuki-Kai. "If I'm not there, they'll miss me; it's an important part." Yuki opened her mouth to protest, but Buffy shushed her.

"It's important, but it's over before the Riding begins. As soon as it's done, I'll come back."

Yuki didn't argue. *She* understood, as almost no other girl in her cohort would have, how unreasonable the Abbess could be, and how cruelly she punished those who would interrupt or delay her dinner, her love-life, her speechmaking. It would be worse for anyone who spoiled her sacred pageant—it would be blasphemy. Bold Yuki felt a stab of fear. "I'll go with you," she started to say.

246

"No; somebody's got to stay here in case Senga comes back. Somebody's got to tell her about Pink and that boy. And let her know there's more of us leaving. You wait here. See if you can find anything to fight with. And I'll be back as soon as I can. Maybe the boy and Pink will come back by themselves. . . I would, if I had a nice house like this."

Yuki nodded agreement. This Buffy was being so grown-up, so sensible—not at all like the stoner, the drunk, the outsider on the edge of the group, whom Yuki had known, she now saw, like the rest of the young ones, only barely.

"Find some food to take with us," this Buffy was instructing, "but not too much. Get water; fill some bottles. If there are knives, get them, too."

Yuki nodded. She thought of the Dangerous Things. She hadn't seen Senga take them.

"I'll be back as quick as I can. Bar the door behind me—do you know how?"

Yuki nodded again, and then Buffy was gone. Yuki watched as her new friend vanished into the fast-approaching twilight. She felt oddly alone as she shut and barred the heavy, oaken door, then turned so her back was against it.

"Right," she said aloud, smacking her hands together. "Food, water, and stuff to fight with."

She didn't know that Senga had taken the most useful and deadly fighting tools to Guatemala, and although Yuki didn't know their names, she kept her eyes peeled for the Dangerous Things as she collected the items that Buffy had told her to gather.

And as she browsed and gathered throughout all the echoing rooms of the Relay Station, rooms that were mostly intact, and rooms that had been stripped to the plaster and lathe for material to shore up the tunnels, a terrible thought occurred to Yuki—what if Pink wouldn't want to leave, now that that man-thing had entered the forest. What if she never saw Pink again, at all?

* * *

Young Parry had seen a naked woman once, in Brooklyn. He had surprised her as she was bathing. She'd made no attempt to cover herself, and he was more alarmed by the fact that the house he'd thought uninhabited was very much otherwise, than by her nakedness—at first. He had broken in through an open upper-storey window, and had planned to let himself out through the front door, downstairs, after he'd had a look around and taken what he wanted. No one in Brooklyn called it burglary; it was survival.

The woman had emerged from her bath and heard the floor creak under Young Parry's feet. She turned to face him down, boldly, with her hands on her ample hips—her tits and her vast belly took their time catching up to the direction of her shoulders As she moved, and as his eyes took in her bulk, she seemed like an ogress to the terrified boy—gigantic and

248

coarse; all blubbery tits and belly, massive thighs, knobby knees and hairy calves, and a substantial thatch of curly hair between her legs that was dripping wet. The look that appeared on the boy Parry's face was such a mixture of horror and revulsion that the naked bather tossed her head back and laughed with a sound like a klaxon. Young Parry heard that laugh ringing in the air behind him as he pelted down the stairs he'd planned to creep down stealthily, and it followed him through the front door and down the alley until he dropped.

In spite of this—and in spite of his feeling for Pink—he had hoped to see naked women again someday; he knew they couldn't all look like the Brooklyn Ogress, as he'd begun to think of her. Nevertheless Young Parry was unprepared for the sight of the women arrayed around the blazing bonfire on the Carousel Lawn as they gathered in readiness for the Snatch, beating makeshift drums and pounding the earth with sticks.

Old women with wiry grey hair on their heads and between their legs, little girls as sleek and shapeless as snakes, girls his own age or a little younger, slim-hipped and narrow-waisted, with strong legs and—and the breasts! Breasts that ballooned and drooped or sat on bellies, or—all milked-out— flattened and stretched over ribs, with dusky nipples the size of pigeons' eggs—or small and solid-looking, barely the size of crab-apples, with blue veins under the skin, and tiny nipples that looked painfully pink and hard. Others were rounded and cup-shaped, with pale nipples that sat up and asked to be sucked. Scooped and floppy, some were almost angular; others like globed fruit. Some sloped, some swelled, and some were hardly there at all in the glare of the firelight. He took a gulp of air and swallowed hard. Without his thinking about it, his hand began traveling toward his once-again rapidly stiffening cock.

"Close your mouth, you'll catch flies," whispered Pink, already possessive and wifelike, beside him.

As he turned to retort, he saw that they were caught. Arrayed behind Pink was a gaggle of naked girls who looked to be about her own age or a little younger, and they were commanded by a puny creature who looked like a rat.

As his eyes adjusted to the darkness away from the firelight's blaze, Young Parry saw that he had been mistaken; these girls were not naked; they had belts made of skin, from which dangled teeth, or finger-bones, or tiny scalps. Before he or Pink could stop her, the rat-girl screamed her piercing scream and kept screaming. She wasn't frightened of them, they realized; she was sending an alarm. Pink noticed, then, that these girls all carried sharpened stakes. She remembered that Young Parry had had a knife—where was it?

As she looked from one to the other of their assailants and then at Young Parry, she hoped that he had read her thought. He nodded his head, slowly, and as he raised his hands in the gesture that in all times and all places means surrender, Pink could see that he must have retrieved his knife and put it in his belt. Why had he let her boss him, them? In spite of the danger they were in, she was forced to smile inwardly, to realize that he had allowed her to think she'd captured him. She inched toward him, all the while watching these girls and their screaming, ratlike leader closely, looking from them to Young Parry and back again.

She now did with her arms what she observed Young Parry doing, and dropping her tree branch she put her hands up, and moved even closer to him. She cowered as if she were more frightened than she was, but also to block the Maenads' view of Young Parry's knife. She hoped he would take the opportunity to use it.

CHAPTER THIRTY

CAGES AND CAPTORS

IN THE YEARS SINCE THE RITUAL OF THE SNATCH BEGAN, IT was not only the pageantry and proceedings that had undergone expansion; there were now scenery, costumes, and, thanks in part to Senga, props.

The rough, slatted crates in which the prisoners were held had evolved. No longer rude wooden pens made of branches lashed together with ropes, they were now more like wooden-wheeled carts surmounted with cages that were themselves festooned with skulls. And not only adult skulls; skulls of the unmourned, unremembered infants who had had the bad fortune to be born male in the forest ornamented the lintels of the cages; the skulls of men served as finials on the corner-posts. Rib bones and pelvises were hammered into the uprights, as were random femurs, tibias, scapulars, sternums, and vertabrae.

Each wheeled cage had a slatted bottom—victims often voided their bowels and bladders before dying, and the slats made the crates somewhat easier to clean. But the bottom of each cage *was* littered—with small bones; carpals, metacarpals, and phalanges from the hands of past victims, cuboids and metatarsals from their feet. Pubic bones, jawbones, kneecaps, and teeth, as well. The bones were thrown there for effect; no one died slowly in the cages, and if they did, their corpses would not have been permitted to repose in the respectful luxury of a slow and peaceful disintegration. The boiled bones of the adult men—the ones that eluded the Abbess's strange addiction—were picked clean and saved for the purpose of adorning the cages; the bones of the male infants were raked out from the pits and ovens every month. Nothing was wasted.

Bone Collector was a Maenad job; slightly higher in status than Cage Cleaner (which was often reserved as a punishment—and one that had been administered to Yuki Kai with a regularity that added fuel to the fire of Yuki's adolescent anger). Thus every girl and woman in the forest had a part in the ritual of the Snatch, and the parts evolved as the particular girls and women changed and grew, or deteriorated and shrank with age and infirmity.

This evening, Mia had been preparing for her part as the Fruits of the Riding, getting into her ropy harness, when her wicked, beady eyes caught sight, in the dusk, of a girl doing nothing. Just staring. With her jaw hanging and her eyes wide open. All the other girls were busy, running to and fro with last-minute preparations. The indolent girl on the opposite side of the Carousel Lawn, intermittently hidden and illuminated by the leaping flames of the bonfire, would spoil everything. Mia grew angry. Everyone should be helping.

There was the ceremonial last meal to be fed to the captives; although the men who had ended up in the cages were usually too terrified to even think of eating or food, it was the job of certain Maenads to poke food at them through the bars. "So it was in the beginning, so it shall be to this day, and for all time," the Abbess had ordered. And Mia always agreed with the Abbess.

Angry Mia told herself she needed to do something. The Snatch had a part for every single woman and girl in the woods, and if a girl was just standing and staring at the fire, as this stupid thing seemed to be doing, then the perfection of the Snatch would be spoiled. It was spoiled already. Mia struggled out of the harness and grabbed one of the sharpened stakes that had been prepared for the ceremony. "Come on," she said to her dresser. "And bring the twins. And be quiet. This should be good!" They sneaked around the long way, staying under the eaves of the trees that ringed the Carousel Lawn, the better to surprise and frighten the lazy thing. They would come at her from behind.

Of course, the idle girl was Pink. Because of some trick of the firelight, or because they weren't expecting to see him, none of the Maenads had noticed Young Parry—until they were facing him. Pink was just raising her hands and moving closer to the young man. She wished—how she wished—that she and Parry had stayed in the Relay Station to wait for Senga that afternoon. She wished she hadn't been so eager to show off for him, to show him the woods as if she knew them better than she really did. She wished she hadn't fought with Senga, and that thought led to this one—where *was* Senga?

The small group of captors seemed more menacing than they actually were; in the leaping firelight they seemed to bristle with spears. Their little rat-faced leader's penetrating screams were piercing Pink's and Young Parry's eardrums, when a deeper voice drowned them out. The voice was familiar to Pink, although its owner was not, as she came suddenly booming through the dusk. With a violent crashing of branches and foliage, a large, loud, grown-up woman wearing a floppy hat and farmer's overalls emerged from the deep woods—"I know her," Pink mouthed to Parry. "I think she's okay."

Pink and Parry huddled together—frozen as much with shock and surprise as with fear—while Buffy, for that's who it was, cheerfully scolded the Maenads who were holding their weapons on the pair. Determinedly ignoring Pink and her young man, Buffy swept past them and scooped Mia up by her naked arm, "What the hell are you doing, Mia? Where's your harness? Come on, it's late!" Grabbing one of the twins by the ghastly belt she wore, Buffy swept her along as well, and her minute-younger sister followed in her wake. "Come on," Buffy turned her head and bellowed back at Mia's dresser—a not-overbright and easily cowed young girl who, with a last, confused look at the captives, scrambled to catch up.

Pink and Young Parry did what Buffy had hoped they would do. After a moment's stunned stillness, they turned and disappeared, running back in the direction the Relay Station, as Mia squealed, "But there's a man, there's a man, there's a man, and a strange girl!"

Buffy stopped, suddenly, and put Mia down on the

lawn without letting go of her arm. The little creature twisted and snarled, but Buffy crooned to her calmly, as if she were years younger, and awakening from a bad dream. A shift in the evening breeze carried smoke from the bonfire toward them, tearing at their throats, stinging their eyes. At some distance away from the fire a chorus of small girls was warming up, singing, "It's catch, before kill . . ."

"Of *course* there's a man, Mia; look, there's two." And Buffy pointed to the terrified men in the cages who were offstage yet, clutching the bars with rigid hands and staring out into the firelit dusk with terrified eyes. Slightly bigger girls, having outgrown the chorus, were poking food at them through the bars, or taunting them by dancing and displaying bare, shapeless backsides to the hapless captives.

"But there was a girl, too, a strange girl . . . " Mia croaked, miserably, as Buffy pulled her along by the arm and shoved her roughly into her dressing chamber behind the Carousel stage.

"I didn't see any strange girl," Buffy lied. "Now c'mon, get into your harness; I've gotta do a safety check before I put you on the rope." She hoped that her diversion had worked. She couldn't afford to look back to be certain; she prayed that Pink and the boy would have had sense enough and time enough to run away while they could. She hoped that if she pretended that she didn't understand what

Mia was saying, that Mia would stop saying it. And in that she underestimated the self-confidence of this small girl who was always believed, because even when she told lies, they were what her listeners wanted to hear.

So Mia kept on, in her penetrating, piercing voice, insisting that there was another man—not just the two in the cages who had been caught days ago and kept alive until now in a pit. Buffy finished fastening Mia's straps and poked her head through the backdrop; the Abbess was pacing before the half-closed curtain like a nervous ingénue from the days when there had been theaters. Rolled up in one hand she carried her script; hands behind her back she was pacing and rapping the palm of her empty hand with the script she held in the other. In the midst of what seemed to Buffy to be scarcely controlled chaos, the Abbess looked to be at peace. She loved this part of the ritual—absorbed in preparation for her role; she didn't look at Buffy, who quickly moved to pull her head back in behind the backdrop, nonetheless.

"Let's see if the pulley works," she was about to say, when she was stricken silent. Even Mia stopped for breath. Across the Carousel Lawn, at the forefront of a spreading wave of sudden silence, strode Hagar and her prey. In the gathering stillness the sound of the bonfire crackled. The flames danced high.

And at the sight of Senga with her head bowed and bloody and her wrists bound, an invisible hand reached its steely fingers into the small of Buffy's back and twisted, hard. The wrench almost undid the muscles encircling her lower back, and the pain reached around to her belly. The resulting spasm almost took the strength out of her substantial legs—however, she managed to keep on her feet. But her breath shuddered out of her slowly and when she could inhale again, it was shallowly, and with considerable pain. Buffy's poor brain, which had already been over-taxed this day, continued to function along the lines of deception, and she recovered enough wit to tell Mia, "I guess you were right" she gulped. "Look. There *is* a man." And she pointed at Old Parry, who was second in line in the unhappy procession, behind Senga.

He had been jabbed and poked with Hagar's sharpened wooden spear for miles and what seemed like many hours. His face was clouded with rage, and every step he took had to be prodded out of him, and so the parade made its way jerkily toward the apron of grass at the front of the stage. Old Parry's back was scratched and punctured where the spears had poked. On seeing the procession, The Abbess rushed forward.

"Praise the Goddess," she cried. "Praise Heavenly Mother!" She dropped her script and clapped her hands together at her breast. "Oh, Hagar—all is forgiven!"

Hagar spat on the ground. She would have a thing or

259

two to discuss with the Abbess tomorrow. She shoved Old Parry forward, and Senga, who was tethered to him, had to follow. The cord between them was short, and pulled her onto her knees. Parry bent to help her up, but was stopped by a Maenad's spear at his chin. Night had fallen, and there was a breeze, but waves of heat from the bonfire washed toward them. The flames provided the only light; in all the excitement, the torches had not yet been lit.

"Attention, girls," the Abbess clapped her hands together and cleared her throat politely. Then something odd began to happen. The girls who had all been looking at Hagar kept looking at her, as if asking for her permission to look at the Abbess. The ones holding the ropes that bound Old Parry looked toward Hagar, as did the ones who held their spears on Senga. The ones across the Carousel Lawn who were piling wood on the bonfire stopped; the ones who were feeding the men in the cages stopped, too. The sluggish torchbearers paused with their torches unlit. The choir stopped singing. The ground was shifting under the Abbess's feet, and as she felt her power draining, she quailed. Her hands flew to her throat.

Hagar stood on the grassy apron before the platform-stage, and stared up at the woman she was about to supplant. It felt good to be acknowledged like this, at last. But the details could wait until tomorrow—there would be changes to the Snatch, starting tonight. Hagar stared at Parry.

"Get another cage," she barked, glancing sidelong at the nearest Maenads. "Where's Buffy? We need her."

Hagar glared at Senga. "We'll deal with you, later, you useless old couze."

With a quick hand motion she ordered two Maenads to tie Senga more soundly. Binding her hands at the wrists and her feet at the ankles, they packaged her into a bundle of pain and propped her against the edge of the stage.

"That's right," said Hagar, bringing her face dangerously close to Senga's, whose mouth was too dry to work up any spit, but whose teeth could still bite.

"We'll let you have a front-row seat." With one foot she delivered a parting kick that caught Senga's rump, before jumping up onto the stage next to the Abbess.

Senga grimaced, and struggled, and writhed, but to little avail. The knots were inexpertly tied, but the cords were tight, and they bound and cut into her, just the same. Her knees hurt where she had fallen next to Old Parry, who was fighting against his bonds, and would have burst them, if not for the spears of the Maenads, some of which were leveled at his throat.

Several of the Maenads had been dispatched to push a

third skull-bedizened cage over the uneven grass and into the center of the Carousel Lawn. They positioned it between the two that were already there and occupied with victims. All three cages now stood between the bonfire and the stage.

Swinging the door of the third cage on its leather hinges and holding it open were two Acolytes. And Parry, stabbed and jabbed with wooden spears and pelted with rocks by a dozen hooting, howling Maenads, was forced inside. As the men on either side of him were doing now, he thundered the bars of his cage and cursed the women. But the little girls dancing around in the firelight like goblins only laughed and showed him their backsides, or laughed and poked him with sticks. They were not cowed.

Buffy, from her makeshift backstage hiding place, had just finished testing the pulley, and had strapped Mia into the harness, ready to fly, when she heard Hagar call her name.

"Coming," she bellowed in Hagar's direction, then turned back to face the still-squalling Mia.

"Sorry," she told her, and slapped the tiny, screeching wretch across the face; hard enough, she hoped, to knock her out. Not hard enough to snap her neck, just enough to shut her up. She pulled on the rope that she'd tested a moment before, and scrawny Mia sailed up into the darkness. Using a snaggled branch behind the open-air stage as a cleat, Buffy fastened the rope and ran, leaving the unconscious rat-girl to swing in the night air, arms and legs dangling, squeaking silenced. Flames from the bonfire licked the night air, and a breaking log spit out a shower of sparks. There was a terrible beauty to them, but it was of a sort that no one in the forest could see.

Chapter Thirty-One

Cages and Captors

A FTERNOON HAD TURNED TO DUSK, DUSK HAD turned to darkness, and Yuki-Kai was close to frantic. She had made up her mind to disregard the plan she'd agreed to with Buffy, and make for the Carousel Lawn by herself. Something had to be very wrong—first Senga had disappeared, and now Buffy was late—and where the hell were Pink and that boy? She couldn't wait—her nerves wouldn't let her. She had to move. Now.

Stepping outside, she pulled the heavy door closed

behind her, and realized that she had left it too late. The sun had gone down and she had no light she could use to guide her through the night woods. Although the darkness held no terror for her, she was as blind anyone else would have been in the black-velvet night. She might miss her friends altogether, and she was equally unhappy in the knowledge that she might run smack into her enemies in the dark. She was stuck; she would have to wait here, until whatever had happened to the others happened to her, too. For she had no doubt by now; something had happened to them.

Her *sang-froid* deserted her, and she began to bite her fingernails. She was just about to break into the supplies that she'd packed into the bags that she'd draped around herself. A candle to use to make a torch of some kind . . . . When suddenly. . . she became aware of a shaft of light, flickering and dancing its way toward her through the woods

Like the finger of sunlight that had illuminated a dusty design inside the Relay Station that afternoon, it was moving, although much more rapidly and without the same expression of purpose. Without knowing why, Yuki hid herself—she wanted to see whoever this was before they saw her.

This was an unknown thing to her, this moving, bouncing light; for when the batteries from the electric torch that had pinned Senga in its beam so long ago had died, they had never been replaced. No one had ever found more, in all their scavenging. Neither Yuki, nor Pink, nor any of the younger Maenads had ever seen a flashlight. There *were* two lanterns, but they belonged to the Abbess and Hagar, who guarded them jealously. Movement at night was almost impossible without light, as Pink had learned, and the power of light was controlled by the Abbess and her lieutenant.

But the light from Young Parry's flashlight, for that's what it was, bounced jauntily as its owner carried it along through the darkness of the rapidly deepening forest night. It did not behave like lantern light; for one thing, it emitted a beam—it didn't glow. When Young Parry passed behind a tree or an overgrown bush, or followed the path he was tracing behind an outcropping, the light disappeared. But it would reappear, denser and brighter, and closer, soon after, every time it did so. And soon, Yuki heard voices. One she recognized, and her heart leapt—the voice she loved best seemed to be giving directions, and the beam of light was bouncing around and in front of her. Pink and the man-boy-thing were coming back to the Relay Station! Yuki couldn't believe her luck.

Her idea of making a torch now abandoned, Yuki rushed from her hiding place to greet them, then hung back at the last instant. She felt shame, recalling how Pink had been balled up and bleeding after their last meeting. But there was no resentment in the way Pink threw her arms around Yuki now, only relief. And Young Parry could only watch and wait. But first there was a confusion of questions that had no easy answers, breathless explanations that didn't explain much, apologies, squeals and many tears.

"Senga and Buffy . . ."

"What happened to you?"

"I'm sorry,"

"It's nothing; a scratch,"

"Who is this?"

"You go first."

Tired of waiting, Young Parry spoke up. "My name's Royston Parry, and I think we should get back inside." He pointed to the Relay Station. "All those women" he gestured with his thumb in the direction from which he and Pink had just come ". . . they might come looking for us." Yuki nodded grimly, seeing the sense of this suggestion, and Pink beamed up at Young Parry as if he had discovered fire.

The little trio moved back toward the door of the Relay Station, which they had barely managed to shut behind them when the "thwock" sound of an arrow thudded against the door. Seconds later, the head of another arrow had buried

267

itself up to its shaft in the wood. The three young ones scrambled to shoot the heavy bar across the door. Another arrow fell uselessly.

"Shit!" the three looked at each other in alarm. The only thought that occurred to any of them was to barricade the door, and this they tried to do as a fourth arrow crashed against the window, breaking the pane through which Yuki and Buffy had spied on the young lovers that afternoon. Grabbing anything they could, furniture, mattresses, crockery, bottles, papers, boxes, old tires, pillows, clothing, and shoes, they threw it haphazardly and futilely against the door, which was now being pried open by Ramona and Alice, the old archers. As Parry had intuited, they had followed the beam of his torch.

They must have brought some kind of prybar, and were enlarging the space between the architrave and the door itself. And although it was stout, the old door was starting to give. The three no-longer-quite-children, Yuki, Young Parry, and Pink, drew close to each other in fear. They had thrown everything they could get their hands on at the door, but of course none of it was any good. Young Parry placed an arm around each girl, Yuki under his right arm, Pink under his left. The only sounds were their ragged, panting breaths, and the horrid squeaking of the door as the prybar did its work. Seconds passed, and before they could recover enough courage to turn and run out the back door, or at the very least try to hide in some corner, the door was almost shattered by a bigger thwock! Pink screamed, and Young Parry covered her eyes with his hand, but Yuki said "Listen. Wait."

Pink pushed Young Parry's protective fingers away from her face, and scowled up at him.

A spear had shuddered into the door of the relay station, flames sprouting from the end of its shaft. It had passed through Renee's chest, pinning her to the wood, bursting her heart. Her dying screams mingled with the screams of terror emitted by Alice as she retreated back towards the Carousel Lawn. She screamed anew some minutes later when she fell blindly into a pit; then she screamed no more.

It was some minutes before the not-children could bring themselves to creep out the back door and around the building to see who or what had saved them. But all they saw when they came around the garden wall was the horrid thing that had been the Acolyte and archer Renee, quite horribly dead and already starting to shrivel as she burned. Both Pink and Yuki surprised Young Parry as they stared at the horror with equanimity. They were not like Brooklyn girls, after all.

"Look," said Pink, pointing to the spear.

The shaft was like that of any of the other spears wielded by anyone else in the forest; at one end their weapons were simply sharpened wooden stakes; effective against the flesh of small animals, suitable for prodding the men caught for the Snatch out of their pits and into their cages, but utterly unable to bury themselves in a wooden door as this one had done. The young ones edged closer to the pinned corpse that had been Renee, eager to see what had had given this spear its lethal heft. Pink nudged Yuki, but there was no need. She, too, had seen the bayonet affixed to the shaft of the stake and buried in Renee's back.

"One of the Dangerous Things," Pink whispered, almost reverently.

Yuki nodded.

"Dangerous Things?" Parry asked.

Both girls looked at him, but Yuki spoke.

"There were three Dangerous Things in a box in the Relay Station. We," she indicated Pink with a jerk of her head, "don't know what they were called. Someone must've stuck this metal knife-thing onto a regular spear, and smeared the spear with fat, and set it on fire."

"Who would do something like that?"

"I dunno."

"Her mother?" He indicated Pink, who shook her head no.

"It's not that she wouldn't," she began to say, intending to defend Senga's honor, but she was interrupted.

"Her mother went to Guatemala this afternoon," Yuki said, unhelpfully as far as Young Parry was concerned. Pink, whose eyes had never traveled far from his face since she had met him, noticed his puzzlement. She shook her head at Yuki. It would take too long to explain. She turned to Young Parry.

"I'll tell you later," she said.

"Anyway, I looked all over for the Dangerous Things this afternoon, and I couldn't find them. They're not in the Relay Station."

"Where could they be, then?"

"Yeah, it'd be nice to know . . ."

"I'm getting to that part. Senga said she was going to Guatemala to let the women there know we were leaving the forest. *She* must've taken the Dangerous Things, and she probably gave the Dangerous Things to them. They can't stand the Abbess, or Hagar, or any of the others. They call

271

them *las mujeres malas*. Bad women."

"And if they're friendly with Senga . . ."

"Then maybe they're friendly to us. Actually, I think they just want us to leave them alone. All of us. But especially the ones they call the bad women. Anyway," Yuki paused. With a glance, she indicated the burning body stuck to the door, "whoever did *this* is a friend to us."

"How do you know it wasn't her mother?"

"Cause her mother wouldn't be hiding from us. Whoever threw this is gone."

Young Parry cast the beam from his flashlight around, illuminating the tree trunks and bushes all around them. The woods, at least as far as his flashlight's beam could reach, were empty.

As he clicked off his torch, the flames from the throwing end of the spear continued licking their way along the shaft of the spear itself, working their way toward the wood of the door. There was plenty of light to see by here. But the hair of Renee's head was burning and giving off a noxious, sulfurous smell. The flakes of paint that were left on the old door began to bubble. The heat the fire gave off was immense; and as Renee's scalp began to cook, the smell of it became odious, as well.

"I think we'd better get back to the Carousel Lawn," said Yuki. "I have a feeling that's where we'll find Senga and Buffy. They're probably in bigger trouble than us." She began to strip off some of the bags she had slung around herself, and was handing them to the others.

"Bigger than getting shot at with arrows?" Young Parry was incredulous. If there were any kind of trouble bigger than this, he didn't want to get any nearer to it. He almost said, *I need to get back to my dad; he'll be worried.*

"It's just because they saw *you*, " said Yuki, matter-of-factly, and as patiently as she could, but finding it hard to be patient when explaining something that should have been so obvious. Pink agreed.

"They probably just wanted to ride you and eat you. They shoot men with arrows all the time, here."

Yuki nodded.

Parry gulped. "That's another thing. What is all this 'riding' and 'eating' stuff?"

Pink picked up one of the bags Yuki had taken off and handed it to Young Parry. "I'll explain while we walk. But Yuki's right. We should go now."

"Can I ask one more question?"

"Depends."

"Were the other 'Dangerous Things' like that one?"

Pink and Yuki spoke at once, words tumbling over each other's as they described the metal balls with the handles and the rings. Young Parry understood, and smiled.

"Hand grenades," he said. "They're called hand grenades. You're right; they are dangerous." He slipped the bag Pink had handed him onto his shoulder.

"And that," he pointed toward the door, where only the charred stump of the spear was left and the shriveled remains of Renee were beginning to spit and crackle, "Is a bayonet. I'd say it was a good one."

At a crashing sound in the underbrush they realized their vulnerability, but for once that afternoon, they were in luck. It was only Buffy.

Chapter Thirty-Two

To the Carousel Lawn

ACH ONE LADEN WITH A BAG OF THE HAPHAZARDLY-
gathered supplies, the group of four pounded back up
the trail toward the Carousel Lawn. Although the three
young ones, helped by Young Parry's flashlight, could
have sped there and back in less than an hour, they
were slowed by Buffy's exhaustion and her age—as well as
by the fact that she had made the trip at least once before, that
busy afternoon.

She was easily winded anyway, due to her years of
weed-smoking and her fattening home-brew drinking, and she

was old. Yet as they traveled, the young ones insistently plied her with questions, taxing her speed and her breathing all the more. From her answers and from their own knowledge, they pieced together what had happened that day. By the time they reached the fringe of the Carousel Lawn, each had a good idea of the trouble they were all in, and Buffy had a stitch in her side, as well, and a desperate need for a drink.

"Wait up," she admonished, and collapsed cross-legged onto the pine-needle carpet under an aging and stately conifer whose topmost branches were sighing in the night wind. For long moments she breathed in and out raggedly, until the young ones finally realized she was not just being lazy old Buffy; she was truly almost spent. And they still had a fight before them, from the looks of things they could see around the bonfire. The taunts and shouts of the Maenads carried across the lawn, and the choir was singing its horrible little anthem that sounded like "Blueberry Hill."

Pink flopped down in front of Buffy and pulled off the older woman's boots. She began to rub her feet. Young Parry flapped his gathering bag back and forth near Buffy's face, fanning her until the sweat on her mounded forehead and her upper lip was well dried. Sensing what was really needed, Yuki thrust one hand into the bib of Buffy's overalls and retrieved the bottle that was stowed there. It still contained a dram, maybe more. She uncorked it and put it to Buffy's lips.

"Look" said Young Parry, pointing across the Lawn.

He had spotted his father.

"Oh, my God," he gasped.

"Goddess," corrected Yuki and Pink, at once. Young Parry ignored them.

Buffy roused herself. "You *know* him?" she asked Young Parry, who did not answer but continued to peer at the man being led toward the middle cage. Slowly, he nodded, but said nothing.

Pink left Buffy's side and stood next to Parry, being careful to stay within the penumbra of the sheltering pine. She peered across the firelit Carousel Lawn. Beside her, Young Parry looked stricken—she tried to follow his gaze. She saw, to cheers and shouts from Maenads and Acolytes alike, the central cage rocked, as a man was shoved inside. But this man looked old. Even Pink could tell he was old; but she supposed it was all right. Until Young Parry almost shouted "That's my father!" and Yuki, next to him, pointed, and whispered, "Holy Mother—that's Senga!"

Young Parry's head whipped around.

"Your Mom?" he demanded. Pink nodded.

"Where?" Buffy had gotten her shoes back on and collected herself. She joined the group at the edge of the lawn.

"Up against that platform-thing."

And then they all saw her—Senga the crone, Senga the recluse, Senga the outcast, the strange, the eccentric, the witch. She had lost that day whatever power she had found in her preserved isolation, it seemed, and was bundled up like household refuse someone had leant against a wall before throwing it away. Some of the smaller girls had stopped pelting the men in the cages with stones, and were starting on her; her arms were bound behind her and she couldn't prevent them. Her blood-smeared head lolled against the platform where the pageant should have been taking place. Of course, this, in some ways, was better than the script-and-costume playacting which the Abbess had contrived. This was real.

But unseen and unsuspected by the Meanads, the Acolytes, the caged men, the Abbess, and Hagar, Senga had found a weak spot and was surreptitiously loosening her bonds. And when Hagar jumped down off the platform to put her face close to Senga's again, she was unprepared for what Senga had planned.

Chapter Thirty-Three

Glasgow Kisses

THE PROBLEM WITH THE GLASGOW KISS, AS SENGA HAD been taught to call it by her father long ago, is its potential for disabling not only the intended target, but the assailant delivering the blow, as well. It is a desperate maneuver, designed for desperate situations. Senga's options were limited; and she had no idea that help was at hand. She might have waited longer, feigning unconsciousness against the platform they called a stage, had she known that four rescuers were at that moment feverishly deciding on the best ways to save her and Old Parry.

But that she did not know—what she knew was that

she had to free Old Parry and herself, collect Pink and Yuki if they could, and once-and-for-all get out of the madder madhouse this forest had lately become. She balked inwardly for a moment at the thought of what she was about to do, but if the situations were reversed, she knew, Hagar would have done it to her.

And so when Hagar, filled with the pleasure of her malice, and enjoying her moment of ascendancy, jumped down off the platform and put her face near Senga's to whisper some small, cruel, indecent thing, Senga simply waited. She balanced herself, getting a good grip of the earth with her feet flat under her haunches, but she feigned defeat, hanging limply forward, until the crown of her head was grazing Hagar's chest. This posture also served to contract her stomach muscles and round out the curve of her back. She would have to hook her head around, she calculated, as Hagar approached her right ear, and she would have to just count on the shock of seeing their leader laid flat to take care of the Maenads; for a moment at least. But a moment was all she would need, she believed.

Heavenly Mother, help me.

And as Hagar came close, Senga exploded upwards, springing from her calves and thighs, ignoring the pain in her recently injured knees, adrenalized and erupting into the side of Hagar's head with a perfectly landed, rising head butt. As she had thought it would, the resulting sight of their prostrate and unconscious leader stunned her followers into silence.

280

And the sight of the furious, fighting Senga sent the smaller Maenads running back to the schoolbuses to put on some clothes. They were suddenly tired of playacting.

Then several things happened at once. From their hiding place under the great pine tree the four rescuers burst across the Carousel Lawn; each young one had at least one knife, and Buffy and Pink brandished their walking sticks. Having emptied the bottle she'd brought with her, Buffy held it by the neck and smashed it against a rock; the crystalline edges made it better than a knife for close-quarters fighting. "No way we're gonna surprise them anyway, and we wanna let your parents know we're coming; so yell your heads off," she had told them. "Let's go!"

So they ran, and raged, raising an inarticulate war-cry of pain and anger, and as they raced past the bonfire, Yuki grabbed at one of the split logs that formed the bonfire skeleton. She managed to catch hold of it in both hands. Still running, she swung it in an arc around her head, and was nearly carried off by the momentum of her swing, but she frightened a good few of the remaining Maenads, and some of the Acolytes, as well, into frozen, paralyzed panic. Pink began to grab rocks from the outer circle that contained the bonfire, and heave them into the small clusters of women and girls who were leaderless and frozen with shock. Several screamed and fell. The rocks were scorching hot and burned Pink's palms and fingers, but she had learned well from Senga to ignore pain. The Pain Game had served her well in the past, and it seemed to be helping her again.

Senga, although momentarily confused and dazzled from the force of the head butt, quickly realized what was happening. With a momentary glance back at the still-lifeless form of Hagar, whom she expected any instant to see rising to her feet, her immediate impulse was to grab and chastize Pink, but she came quickly to her senses and made for the cage containing Old Parry instead. She reached it at the same moment Young Parry did, and assumed that he was a prisoner who'd also escaped. Together they fumbled with the leather thongs that were almost better than metal locks; it was nearly impossible to break or pry the sinewy substance apart, and it was not until Senga noticed the knife at Young Parry's waist and grabbed it that they were able to slice and saw open the leathery lock that held Old Parry captive.

If there was one thing Old Parry was good at, it was surviving. He knew when to fight, and when to run; and this was a time for both.

"YOU!" He roared at his son. "I'll deal wi' you later! Come on!" and he sprang from the cart-bed onto the dry grass between the cage where he'd been so briefly held captive and the stage where the deranged figure of the Abbess was running back and forth uselessly. Senga ran in the opposite direction, toward where Pink was still pelting Maenads with rocks before they could get too close to her with their spears. Truthfully, there were not many Maenads left in the bonfire clearing now, and when Senga reached her daughter she spent

282

some moments getting her arms around her, calming Pink and stopping her from a fruitless expenditure of more energy. Most of their enemies had scattered in panic; but there was no telling when they'd gather their courage and their wits and come back to re-engage them.

Taking back his knife, Young Parry sliced open the leather thongs that fastened the cages of the other men—but if he was looking for them to help their side, he was disappointed. They vanished as soon as they could get their legs under them. Whether they knew a way out of the forest or not, they disappeared, noisily, into the night and didn't look back.

Young Parry ran after his father, who had sprung up onto the platform to face the Abbess. She had stopped running around like a rabbit and had grabbed a small Maenad by the shoulders. She held the terrified child in front of her, as a shield.

If Senga had felt a momentary hesitation before dispatching Hagar, Old Parry felt nothing of the sort when face-to-face with the Abbess, whom he recognized as the author of his anger and fear. She and these women she controlled had killed the young men of Brooklyn, the sons of his friends and neighbors. And they would have killed his son, too. For himself, he wasn't angry, and he wasn't really afraid to die. But he wanted his son to live.

As he advanced on the Abbess, he reached forward and unhooked her fingers from the shoulders of the terrified child she held before her, and pushed the little girl behind him, towards his son. The Abbess's mouth was moving but no words were emerging from between her dry lips. She retreated and Old Parry advanced.

The combination of blows that Old Parry was planning to land on her had been referred to at one time as the "one-two," in the sport of boxing, in which the old man had excelled in his prime. He took the Abbess's measure with a glancing left-handed tap, then smiled his grim smile as he followed it up quickly with a substantial left jab and a swift right cross. The Abbess's mouth stopped moving. She went down like a sack of meal. Blood dribbled out of her split lips and stained the yoke of her white garment, onto which also dropped a tooth, with a fragment of gum attached. She lay where she'd landed and didn't move.

"Right," the old man turned and bellowed at his son, in whose brotherly embrace the small girl was still sheltering. Noticing the terrified child, Old Parry modified his tone. "You and me," he snarled at the boy, and if the small, frightened child cowering between them did not understand what he meant, Young Parry did. He gulped, and opened his mouth to offer a defense, when an explosion knocked everyone—man, woman, son, daughter, Maenad, Acolyte, and outsider off his or her feet. For some moments, each lay stunned and puzzled, before adrenaline got them moving again.

"What the hell was that?"

"I'll tell ya later, Pop," said Young Parry, although he

thought he knew.

The Guatemalans had unleashed one of the Dangerous Things, aiming at, and evidently hitting, the center of the bonfire.

Fragments of the grenade shell combined with the shrapnel it had contained, and with a shower of great clods of dirt and fiery logs; the bonfire had exploded. Seconds later, as the rain of fire plummeted down around them all, a second explosion further away in the dark tore open the Carousel. And soon, it was clear that the forest was burning.

"Come on, Pop," said Young Parry. "You can yell at me later."

The two men picked up the terrified child between them, each holding one of her arms, and ran in the direction they had last seen the others. If they stayed together they might be able to find their way out before the forest fire devoured them all.

Chapter Thirty-Four

Wind and Flame

WHAT SOUNDED LIKE WIND FOR A BRIEF MOMENT, BUT WAS really the sound of the forest devouring itself in flame, grew in immensity and began to chase the fighters across what was left of the Carousel Lawn.

The Lawn—as the fighters could now see in the violent firelight—was being roiled and riven from beneath as if some monstrous underground burrowers, gargantuan moles or snakes, had suddenly wakened from long hibernation and gone desperately, purposefully, to work, tunnelling. Or it may have been the roots of the trees around the lawn, waking angrily and bursting to take vengeance on those who had so badly abused their hospitality. Whatever the cause, the very soil the fighters stood on was unquiet, as it hadn't been since the long-ago day of the crash.

The sound of the wind built on itself and grew louder and darker, and more and more intense, and the earth under the fighters' feet began to become furrowed and folded. It tumbled them over and over amid the sounds of crackling and breaking that accompanied the growing inferno, until they lost all chance to regain their footing. When that happened, they had no choice but to let themselves be carried along atop a rolling wave of earth. It carried them forward and funneled them onward, faster and harder toward the mouth of the last tunnel that Senga had built. And there it deposited them, shaken but unhurt.

And as a householder might shake a sheet to make a bed, the forest floor shook itself smooth again, and became still. The tumbled fighters arose unsteadily, sore, in mind and body, from all they'd endured in the last hours, but alive. The tunnel mouth yawned before them. The earth at their feet gave one last little hiccup before smoothing itself into something that looked like a threshold.

Get inside.

The voice spoke to each of them, Senga, Buffy, Yuki, Pink, and both Parrys. But no one had uttered a word. They looked at each other for some minutes, puzzled.

In the distance, children were crying. Their high-pitched keening could be heard like a whining descant above the deepening music of the forest on fire. Smoke was beginning to blur the fighters' vision and sting their eyes. Their throats were becoming raw.

"Some of those Maenads were pretty small," croaked Yuki, staring at the tunnel mouth.

The others shook their heads in agreement, but they hesitated. Forward, or back?

"They don't sound too far away," said Yuki. "I'll see if I can get them to follow me," and before they could stop her, her bounding, vital, animal step had carried her back into what was left of the woods. The remaining trees in their now sparse but orderly avenues seemed ready to snatch at her, but either because she was too quick, or because the will of the forest approved of her, or for some other reason, they allowed her to pass. But they didn't let any of the others, who were ready to do so, follow her. The fighters wasted several uncertain moments looking at each other.

And the roaring fire-sound, the crackling and snapping of it, was now combined with the angry war-cries of the women who had been the Acolytes. They were coming.

Get inside.

No one had spoken. But each heard the voice.

Senga was gripped by her old fear, and stood at the tunnel mouth for long seconds, dread etched on her features.

"I could wait here for Yuki," she started to say.

"Naw, Hen. This forest knows her. The forest will see her right. C'mon." Old Parry took her by the elbow.

"I don't fancy havin' tae fight that lot a second time,"

he explained. "Let's go."

And as he spoke, he extended his hand for his torch—his flashlight—which his disobedient son had clipped to his own belt the previous night. Old Parry knew of Senga's fear of dark places and small spaces. He would light her way into the tunnel. Much more than that he couldn't do. But he would do what he could.

So Young Parry handed over his father's torch, and began paying out the length of rope that he'd carried, over his shoulder, under his arm, and across his chest since his part in this adventure began, back in Brooklyn. The screeches of the Acolytes grew louder, and were then drowned out again by the ongoing roar of the flames.

"Put your arms up over your head," Young Parry told Pink, who looked puzzled. But Buffy understood what Young Parry meant to do. She nudged Pink, and put up her own arms.

"Do like this," she said, "quick," and Pink understood. Young Parry began linking them together with the coil of rope. He left a length at the front of the line for himself, and at the back he tied the rope around his father's waist. There wasn't quite enough for Senga.

"I'll take charge of her," said Old Parry, at which Senga bridled.

"I'm all right."

"Certainly, that you are," he exhaled. "Now, move," and he gestured with the flashlight.

Senga took one last look back at the burning forest,

and with a deep breath, plunged into the dark.

* * *

It was worse than she remembered. There was of course the familiar fetid smell of the inhabited earth, and the crepitating sounds of the beasts that lived there. Old Parry noticed her start with alarm and he also noticed the cause; a tiny greenish pair of glowing eyes reflected in the flashlights' beams. It was joined by another pair, and then another.

"Close your eyes, I've got you," he whispered. She tried this for a few steps, but of course it was useless. Making her way, even in the dark, with only one good eye, was better than attempting to navigate blind. Anyway, the beasts were still there, even if she couldn't see them. She could hear them shrilly squeaking. She opened her eyes again quickly and squeezed Old Parry's hand. They moved awkwardly on together into the darkness. The rest of the fighters were stumbling forward in front of them. They went sideways, like crabs, stooped and half-crawling through the shaft that Senga had only made big enough for a woman and child to fit into and through. The fighters' breathing was rapid and loud, a contrast to their progress through the darkness, which was silent and slow. Moment piled on moment, and the faster they tried to proceed, the more slowly it seemed they managed to go. But they progressed.

Of the cave-in that had driven her out of the shaft the last time she'd worked it, there was no evidence; no mound of loose earth to push away, and this puzzled her until she told herself that if the forest floor could crease and uncrease itself like a sheet, it could clear away a pile of loose earth in a tunnel with no problem.

So there was that to be thankful for.

She began to tick things off in her mind; they had a source of light—not wavering fat-candle flames that flickered and threatened to go out at the whisper of a subterranean breeze, but yellow torchlight that was steady and regular.

And she was not alone; even if she were to die here, underground, someone would take care of Pink. Death was the obsession that had always tormented her in the tunnelly dark; death, and worse than death; burial alive, to feel herself being eaten by the beasts that crept and crawled across her skin, bitten by the spiders whose webs brushed against her face and arms, gnawed upon by the rats whose whiskers she could feel tickling her skin—voracious rats with their malicious appetites—and her, powerless to do anything to stop them. Senga's breath came quicker—now that her imagination had been unleashed, her memory was sure to follow.

Memory of darkness and squeezing; a fumbling, jabbing, horrid something she didn't understand. A mouth on her mouth, a rough beard scratching her cheek in the dark of the dangerous basement, and herself small and powerless. The hand that gripped her heel from behind was almost welcome; it placed her fear outside herself once more. Old Parry's hand had slipped out of hers moments before as he moved forward, and she heard behind her the voice of her enemy whisper her name.

"Take me with you," it muttered.

Senga turned. There was just enough light from the flashlights ahead of her to see there was someone else in the passage with her. She grew courage from anger and hissed.

"Sorry, sister. No can do," and jumped forward onto her pursuer with her nails ready. She gouged and grappled. She silently choked and strangled her foe until Old Parry—having realized what was happening—turned back to help, only to find his help wasn't needed. He was too late either to aid Senga or to save her adversary.

"She's finished," he told her. "Let her go. Enough."

Senga stared at him like a sleepwalker, her hands still tight around her enemy's throat. "Enough?"

"Aye," he answered. The woman crumpled at their feet certainly looked dead.

"Come on." He shook Senga's shoulder. "Well done. Come and see; you got farther than you realized; we're almost oot."

She let him take her hand again and moved forward, and left her fear in the tunnel with her dead foe.

She saw that Old Parry had not been joking, nor had he been pacifying her; a dim glow that was not artificial torch light was creeping into the tunnel and spreading toward them. Daylight.

"Come on" yelled Young Parry, tugging on the rope

that joined him to Pink

"I can't believe it," yelled Buffy, as a vast, man-made shape came into sight. But really, she did believe it.

The dim light of day was being filtered through something Senga, Old Parry, and Buffy recognized at once.

"I knew it," Senga whistled. But she had only surmised; she hadn't known.

Before them, as if it had been lodged there by the force of the original disaster, was the end compartment of a New York City subway train. It blocked the end of the tunnel just a few yards on from where Senga had stopped digging years ago. Buffy's massive hands had moved the rest of the earth; Young Parry and Pink had dispersed it. Old Parry had untethered himself and come back to look for Semga.

"I knew the subway was near this part of the park," Senga told him, proudly. Her face, like his, was streaked with soot and gleaming with sweat and exhilaration.

"Well, what's a subway, and what good does that do us?" Young Parry and Pink looked dismayed.

"I'll show you what good," said Buffy. "Get this rope off me. Give me a boost," She and the two other old ones were excited. Senga and Old Parry understood what she intended to do. They had traveled by subway many times in their youths; perhaps in this very car. Certainly they had traveled on this line.

Old Parry nudged his son. "Bend down."

Young Parry did as he was told, forming with his bent

back a stepping stool for Buffy to climb up on.

"Sorry," she said, as he winced under her weight. She stepped off his back as quickly as possible—hauling on the grab iron outside the car door, she yanked her bulk off his back and up onto the connector platform. She bent her knees and bounced, mimicking the motion the car would have made as it rolled along the tracks. The rubber-sheathed chains that were supposed to prevent passenger accidents were still there.

"Like old times," she grinned. "Smokin' and ridin' between the cars!"

Old Parry shone his flashlight beam onto the door of the car. "Just see if you can get that door open, or it's gonna be a long road back, with a fight at the end of it."

Senga shuddered.

"Get it open, Buffy. Please."

The sliding handle was rusty, and it squealed when Buffy gripped it, but it didn't budge, as hard as she pushed and pulled. She put her broad back into it, but it was no use; the lock wouldn't move, the handle was frozen.

"Up you go, lad," Old Parry nodded to his son. He helped Buffy back down onto the tunnel floor, where she stood next to Senga, whose arm crept around her shoulders.

But he had no better luck than Buffy. Senga looked back into the darkness from which they had come; she heard something. Pink was clasping her hands and bouncing on the balls of her feet.

"You can do it, Royston," she called up to him.

294

"Royston?" the three adults cried, as Young Parry gave a last, heroic pull, assisted by the surge of adrenaline and embarrassment at Pink's use of his first name.

"Got it," young Parry grunted. The door of the car slid open.

"Almost there," said Buffy and Senga at once. Young Parry leant down and gave Pink a hand up onto the platform.

"Do me a favor," he said. "Don't call me Royston."

He turned to his father.

"Aren't trains supposed to have tracks under them?" he asked.

Old Parry nodded, clambering up onto the platform himself.

"It must have jumped them."

Young Parry hadn't any idea of the behavior of trains and their tracks. He shrugged.

"How many compartments do you think there are?" asked Buffy, helping Senga up and into the car.

"We'll soon find out," said Old Parry. "Close that," he nodded at the sliding door.

"No," Senga called. "Leave it. . . . Yuki."

"Aye. . . . Right."

"What'll we do if the other end is stuck," asked Buffy, making her way down the aisle, swinging from handrail to handrail like the schoolgirl on a trip to the city that she had once been.

Old Parry grinned.

"'In case of emergency, break glass.'" He pointed to the compartment windows.

"We'll find out."

Young Parry gripped the cold, brass, L-shaped handle on the door at the end of the car and jerked it to the right, then the left. The door, untried for thirty years or more, slid violently and unexpectedly open with the strength of Young Parry's arm. The fighters crowded together in the aperture, gazing with mouths open and eyes wide at the strange sight that lay before them. Pink jumped down from the small lip at the edge of the door. The old ones helped each other down.

They were in a cavernous, echoing space, with half-tiled walls and standing pools of water inches deep in places on the uneven concrete floor. It smelled yeasty and dank. There were twisted things the old ones knew were girders, and hanging things the old ones knew had been lamps. Metal bars outlined a kind of cage, and a flight of stairs, through which pale early morning light was glimmering led up and out. A subway station. Senga thought she might weep. Old Parry wiped his nose. Only Buffy seemed unaffected.

"Leave that torch here," Old Parry told his son. "And leave it on. Yuki might yet find her way."

They walked on trembling legs from the connector platform onto the floor of the station, and began the walk up the stairs into what, they did not know.

CHAPTER THIRTY-FIVE

QUEENS

"I THINK WE MIGHT HAVE MADE A BIG MISTAKE," said Senga, as with a gravid, sonorous, roaring "whoomp," the eaves of the forest, which they could just see behind them, were consumed in a surging sheet of orange flame. Smoke billowed towards the escapees from the base of the blaze, and the heat wave fried the small hairs on their forearms immediately. The force of the heat pushed Senga back around. She faced the empty avenue of torn and jumbled asphalt paving lined with rusting, long-abandoned automobiles that stretched before her, and which she vaguely thought she recognized. Young Parry was helping his father up the last steps and onto the pavement that opened before them. And Pink and Yuki-kai were holding each other up and coughing, black clods of dirt stuck to their skin and hair. *She made it,* Senga told herself.

Before them, the landscape dipped slowly away to what they thought might be the east, a dim, grey grassland studded with the broken pillars of old, elevated roadways and the roots of tenements. The hot wind from the burning forest picked up intensity; it gusted toward them and pulled down a faded metal street sign. Buffy bent down and picked it up. The lettering on it could still be read, only barely. There was a capital "Q," and an "n," and a "d." "Queens Boulevard?" several voices guessed at once.

"Let's get away from here," said Senga, as bits of breeze-blown ember lighted on her hair. "That way." She was pointing toward a long, low, brick building lying in a shallow grassy declivity; there were no panes in any of the window frames, but the structure seemed largely intact. "Let's see if they'll let us stay there. . . . "

"First, let's find out if there's any 'they' there," said Buffy, quite sensibly, for a change. *Everyone is changing,* thought Senga. She and Buffy began to herd the others towards the less broken parts of the roadway that had evidently been Queens Boulevard. As far as they could tell, they were alone; there was no sign of human habitation. Aside from the vast, rumbling note of the fire, there was silence. Not even a scrap of paper was left after all the years of ruin to blow itself against their legs; everything that could blow had already blown away.

Senga began to count the survivors. Herself, Old Parry, Young Parry, Pink . . . *and where had Yuki-Kai disappeared to?* Senga's heart seemed to catch and stop for a full count of ten, and then she saw the girl, walking out of the still-smoking tunnel mouth with a smaller girl on her shoulders, and another holding her hand. Several more small heads bobbed into view behind them, coming up out of the tunnel and into the weak, grey, early morning light.

She got them out, said Senga to herself, and smiled.

"She got them out."

She looked at Pink, who was lingering near the tunnel entrance, peering back inside, holding hands out to the last of the Maenads, choking on smoke.

"Pink," Senga called, hands cupped around her mouth. "Come away from there. Ask Yuki if any of the Guatemalans got out."

Yuki had heard her, and shook her head, no. Senga sighed, and bowed her head.

She turned to face Old Parry, who had come up behind her and had slipped his hard hand into hers in the smoke-stained morning. Another moment passed, and the sudden sunrise broke the back of the night. The dawn that erupted was pearl-colored, and pink, and gold, in the distant sky and all around them as well. Jangled notes from a wild chorus of strange birds met their ears. Parry smiled, but his smile was tired and grim. "Well," he said, "Are ye dancin'?"

Senga smiled back wearily; she knew the answer—the only answer.

"Are ye askin'?"

"Aye, I'm askin,'" said Parry, grasping her around the middle, and pulling her close against him, squeezing a little too tight.

"Then I'm dancin'," answered Senga, pulling out of his too-tight embrace, but loving the man in whose arms she was content to be captured. She knew he was failing and flawed, but she wanted him anyway, more than she had realized in all the years of their exile. Or perhaps because of all the years of their exile from each other.

And at that moment of incongruous emotion, into all the yielding relief, and the sweetness of vengeance, and the rambunctious wonder at being alive and able still to love that suffused her—an old sensation crept. She recognized it; that finger's touch of dread on the webs that bound her heart. It was that feeling a woman ignores to her peril, but ignore it she does, when she realizes that somehow her life has become yoked to that of another, even a good man, even a loved man. She turned to face her Parry, whose beloved, battered, features were grim and set, whose face was open and strong, determined and hopeful, and she thought, *What have I done now? Goddess, help me—what have I done, now?*

But she shook off the gossamer brush of her fears and gripped Parry's hand obstinately in her own. She smiled at him, and then turned her face toward the glorious ruins of their future. "Yep," she repeated. "I guess we're dancin'."

EPILOGUE

And deep in the dark heart of the forest, to which they had retreated and where they hoped the fire would not reach, something small and wounded scrabbled weakly but purposefully in the dirt, and then stopped, then pulled itself forward, slowly and painfully, moved, and then stopped again. And something scorched and scalded licked its wounds, and sat, and sucked on bones. But that is another story.

Made in the USA
Charleston, SC
19 July 2013